Warrior Rising
PAMELA PALMER

MILLS & BOON

First published in Great Britain 2012
by Mills & Boon,
an imprint of Harlequin (UK) Limited,
Large Print edition 2012
Harlequin (UK) Limited, Eton House,
18-24 Paradise Road, Richmond, Surrey TW9 1SR

ISBN: 978 0 263 23040 6

Printed and bound in Great Britain
by CPI Antony Rowe, Chippenham, Wiltshire

Ilaria stared at him, her heavy-lidded expression stunned and confused.

Her mouth was swollen and damp from his kisses, a perfect rosy pink that had his hands curling around her shoulders, his muscles straining against the nearly overwhelming need to pull her back into his arms.

"What are you doing to me?" In his mind, the words sounded accusatory, but to his ears the question only sounded confused. "You're enchanting me."

She shook her head. Her lips parting as if in denial. But even as Harrison watched, they closed softly on a smile. A sad smile. "You don't want to desire me. But you do."

And she was right. Exactly right. He was a man who valued control above almost anything, yet within moments of meeting her, she'd attacked every ounce of control he possessed, and he'd yet to recover. It was all he could do not to pin her to the wall and take everything she offered.

Which only made him angry. She was the enemy.

Pamela Palmer is a *New York Times* and *USA TODAY* bestselling author. When her initial career goal of captaining starships didn't pan out, Pamela turned to engineering, satisfying her desire for adventure with books and daydreams until finally succumbing to the need to create worlds of her own. She lives and writes in the suburbs of Washington, DC.

Dear Reader,

Finally, I present to you the eagerly awaited conclusion to the Esri series. Although I've taken care to make certain you won't be lost if you start with this book, I hope you'll eventually read the entire series. The first three books of the series, *The Dark Gate*, *Dark Deceiver*, and, most recently, *A Warrior's Desire* are available in e-book formats.

The Esri series has always been very near and dear to my heart. Previously, ex-Navy SEAL, Charlie, discovers a woman of strength, beauty, and passion in the pretty little slave, Tarrys, as they complete a dangerous mission into Esria to rescue the imprisoned Esri princess, Ilaria. Now Charlie's brother, Harrison, whose hatred for the Esri knows no bounds, has been forced to guard the far-too-alluring Princess Ilaria as they struggle to seal the gates between the worlds once and for all.

I hope you enjoy this world and characters as much as I have.

Best always,

Pamela Palmer

Thanks to Laurin Wittig
and Anne Shaw Moran, my critique
partners, my buddies, and the sisters of
my heart. I couldn't do it without you
and wouldn't want to. Thanks, too,
to Ann Leslie Tuttle, Robin Rue,
Kim Castillo, Emily Cotler,
Sarah Drasner, and Dana Hamilton
for all your efforts on my behalf.
I love working with you all.

And thanks and love to Keith for
accompanying me on the research trips
and for always being there for me.
My hero.

Chapter 1

Midnight was still several hours away, the moon full behind a thick layer of snow clouds. Activity around the Dupont Circle fountain in downtown Washington, D.C., buzzed with a grim, almost desperate determination as more than a dozen metropolitan police, wearing wristbands of holly, cordoned off the traffic circle while a team of D.C. firefighters set up the fire ring that would be lit just before the witching hour.

Harrison Rand strode around the circle, over-seeing the activity as the humans busily created a defense against the night's probable coming inva-sion. Every month, for an hour at midnight of the full moon, the gates between the human world and Esria opened. For fifteen hundred years, the

Esri—the man-sized, malicious creatures at the heart of the legends of fairies and elves—had been locked out of the human world, the gates sealed, but for the one forgotten…a gate that opened, oddly enough, into the heart of Washington, D.C.

Six months ago, an Esri had stumbled upon that forgotten gate by accident, on the scent of one of the seven stones of power, and things had gone downhill fast. Now all twelve gates were open and the Esri's King Rith was hell-bent on tearing down the walls between the realms and enslaving the entire human race. Apparently, he had the power to do it. Or he would have, if he managed to get his hands on the magically powerful stones that had long ago been left in the human realm, stones that Harrison and his small team had searched for and found, and now guarded with their lives.

Harrison's sole mission in life had narrowed down to one thing—protecting humanity from the Esri. And the only way any of them could do that was to reseal the gates before King Rith's minions managed to steal back the stones, giving Rith the power he sought. But sealing those gates was a damn sight easier said than done.

He adjusted the combat vest that he'd donned in case the Esri came through shooting arrows this time. Blasted, uncomfortable thing. The CEO of his own computer software company, his world used to be one of the office, his uniform a pair of khakis and a polo shirt. It was his brother, Charlie, who'd always been the soldier, not him. But thanks to the trace of inhuman blood that apparently ran through their veins—Esri blood from some long-ago immortal ancestor—they were both soldiers now.

Those who couldn't be enchanted, the humans with that trace of Esri blood—humans the Esri called *Sitheen*—were the only ones who could fight this war. And the Sitheen numbered only a handful.

As snowflakes began to swirl, his gaze moved to the white marble fountain itself, rising high into the air like a giant chalice. In the summer, water would tumble from that high loft down into the circular base from which the carved pedestal rose.

In the dead of winter, there was no water. If anything moved in that chalice tonight, it would be Esri.

A chill went through him that had only a little to do with the frigid air. He zipped up his parka and listened as Jack and Kade gave last-minute instructions to the five new Sitheen recruits Kade had found at area military installations and police departments.

Jack Hallihan was a D.C. cop, six feet tall, as big or bigger than any of the recruits. Kade, or Kaderil the Dark as he was known in Esria, towered over the lot of them like they were midgets. Seven feet of hard-muscled Esri, the immortal was half-human and didn't look anything like his pale-skinned, pale-haired, slim-built brethren. Thank God for small favors, Kade was on their side now.

Harrison frowned. He didn't want to trust the Esri...*any* Esri. And he definitely didn't want to like this one. But Kade had offered up his immortal life to protect the humans—in particular, Autumn, the human woman he'd fallen in love with. It was hard to hate a guy like that.

But that didn't mean he couldn't hate the rest of the raping, murderous bastards. And he did. He despised them with a fury he sometimes thought would choke him.

Six months ago, an Esri had touched Harrison's seven-year-old daughter, Stephie. He'd just placed his white hand on her head, but whatever he'd done to her had made her scream and scream. And when the screaming had finally stopped, her mind had flown to a place no one could reach. She remained in a catatonic state from which doctors and Harrison's ex-wife feared she might never recover. God alone knew what that monster had done to her. All Harrison knew was that the Esri were powerful, dangerous, magical beings. And he would do everything in his power to stop the bastards. Which meant getting these damned gates sealed again.

For the hundredth time since he'd arrived at Dupont Circle tonight, he pulled out his cell phone, making certain it was still on.

If only Charlie would call. His ex-navy SEAL brother had gone through the gate last month on a Hail-Mary mission to free the captive Esri princess, Ilaria—the one they believed had sealed the gates between the worlds fifteen centuries ago.

To beg her to seal them again.

Dammit, Charlie, call me.

He knew his brother had taken a cell phone. If he came through one of the other gates, he'd call. And considering midnight fell at different times in different places—and they suspected most of the gates opened into northern Europe—that should have happened at least a couple of hours ago.

They thought. They really didn't know squat about these gates.

Come on, Charlie. Call me, little brother. Tell me you and Tarrys got the princess. Tarrys, a pretty little ex-slave from the Esri world had accompanied him through the gate, intending to keep an eye on him. *Tell me you made it out of there alive.*

Jack's wife, Larsen, joined him, her blond hair tucked beneath the hood of her dark green parka. Larsen had been one of the first Sitheen targeted by the Esri, one of the first to understand that the bleached-skinned, murdering rapist she alone saw clearly, wasn't human.

"Any word?" she asked softly. She was an attractive woman. A lawyer, if they ever got their lives back. Jobs no longer meant much when they faced an evil bent on the destruction of their world.

"No. Nothing."

Her hand went to his arm as if he might need some strengthening or commiseration at Charlie's lack of communication, but Harrison was more than used to this. Charlie had always been the more adventurous of the two, even before Dad left on a business trip with his young female assistant and never bothered to come home, propelling Mom into a deep and abiding relationship with the liquor cabinet. Afterward, his brother had turned wild and still seemed to thrive on danger. Harrison had long ago accepted the fact that sooner or later Charlie wouldn't return from one of his missions.

For the sake of the world, he just hoped this wasn't the one.

"Charlie warned it might take time to reach the

princess," Larsen said. "If he doesn't make it out of there this month, he'll come back next."

Harrison nodded once. There was nothing to say to that. Charlie would make it or he wouldn't. Unfortunately, if he didn't return, they might never know his fate. He could be captured and imprisoned. Or enslaved. He could desperately need their help and they'd never know.

As his stomach threatened to turn into a mass of knots, he took a deep breath and forced the tension out with an exhale. In his mind, he retreated to that dark, colorless room devoid of emotion. Another breath. Calm, controlled.

"If it's any consolation, I haven't had any visions."

He met Larsen's gaze, understanding her meaning. Many of the Sitheen seemed to have inherited some kind of fairy gift from their Esri ancestors. Larsen foresaw death, the deaths of other Sitheen. No visions meant Charlie was still alive.

Probably.

"That's something," Harrison murmured.

Larsen gave him a hopeful little smile and turned away. But she'd gone no more than two steps when she suddenly jerked, as if she'd been struck.

Instinctively, Harrison's gaze flew to the gate, assuming she'd seen something. But no dark forms leaped from the base of the fountain. Larsen swayed. Understanding hit him like a body slam. She was having a vision. Larsen was watching someone die.

He grabbed her by the shoulders, steadying her. "Jack!"

Jack Hallihan's dark head snapped up, his body leaping into motion as he ran for his wife. As Jack pulled Larsen into his arms, he looked up, Harrison's own despair mirrored in his eyes. Together, they waited to find out which of them she was watching die.

Please, God, don't let it be Charlie. I can't warn him. I can't help him change his fate. Larsen finally stirred, turning her head to press one cheek against Jack's shoulder, revealing a tear-streaked face as pale as any Esri's.

"What did you see?" Jack asked softly, stroking her cheek with his thumb.

She lifted her hand to cover her mouth, as if

struggling for control, and Harrison knew they weren't going to like the answer. Finally, she pulled out of Jack's embrace and swiped at the tears. Though visibly shaken, the woman was tough. With a deep, shuddering breath, she met their gazes, one after the other.

"I saw ten or twelve slaves come through the gate first, all shooting arrows. Fifteen or twenty Esri flew through after." She opened her mouth to continue, then squeezed her eyes closed as more tears ran down her cheeks.

Jack gripped her shoulder, offering her strength as they both waited silently for her to continue. As bad as Harrison knew her vision had been, one thought kept racing through his head. So far, it was about them, not Charlie. And they could change it.

Larsen got control again and continued, her bottom lip unsteady. "Most of us die from arrows through the neck and head."

"The vests aren't going to be enough," Jack murmured.

"No. And those who don't die from the arrows, will be killed by Esri knives."

Harrison's neck felt stiff as he lifted his gaze to Jack's, seeing in the cop's eyes the same frustration he was feeling. A month's worth of extensive planning and it was all going to be for nothing.

With a rough sigh, Harrison shook his head. "We need a plan B, and fast."

"What about the fire ring?" Jack asked his wife. The firefighters were setting it up, even now. "Does it help at all?"

"I didn't see any fire."

Jack frowned, his gaze returning to Harrison's. "What does that mean?"

"They have to be coming through early."

Alarm flashed in the cop's eyes. "I agree. They could be coming through any minute. And we're going to need additional protection against the arrows." He kissed his wife on the cheek, already springing into motion. "I can get us some helmets. And we'll circle vehicles around the park to act as shields." His voice floated back as he took off toward the police captain.

Harrison squeezed Larsen's shoulder. "Are you okay?"

She met his gaze with traumatized eyes. "It never gets any easier."

Hatred clawed at his insides. "We're going to stop them, Larsen. I swear it." His gut clenched. "You didn't…?" He couldn't finish.

"I didn't see Charlie. I think I would have, Harrison. I think I'd know if he'd died. He told you he'd return with a fairy princess on his arm, didn't he? We have to believe he will. Princess Ilaria is our only hope."

For the hundredth time, he thought of that painting some nineteenth-century Sitheen had painted of a woman he'd never known, a woman Kade later confirmed was Princess Ilaria. That pale, pale skin and hair. Those bright green eyes. If she weren't Esri, he might have thought her beautiful.

She was their only hope. An *Esri* was their only hope, and what did that say about their chances of success?

That they were next to zero, that's what. His fingers curled into fists inside his pockets.

Even if the Sitheen resistance survived the night's battle, they were in deep trouble.

He reached once more for his cell phone.
If only Charlie would call.

Princess Ilaria stood in the dark field beneath a sky filled with a million stars, and saw nothing but the fire branded onto the backs of her eyelids and seared into her brain. Memories, just memories, but she shook just the same. The flames circling her, creeping up her gown, crawling over her fingers and hands, burning the flesh from her bones. Not real memories, for the fire had never been real, only visions the Forest of Nightmares had created for her, had brutalized her with. Visions that bombarded her mind, still, although she was finally free of that miserable place.

The icy wind tore at her gown, snowflakes stinging her face and hands even as perspiration rolled between her shoulder blades. With a violent shudder, she fought the clawing memories, pushing them back, trying to grasp the fact that after three hundred years, she was finally free of the prison King Rith had consigned her to. A place she'd feared she'd never leave.

Long, curly hair blew into her face, yet she

could do nothing but turn her head to escape the blowing locks. Her shaking hands were still tied firmly behind her back. She willed her heart to cease its terrible pounding. There was no fire here. Not yet, though she knew the human realm to be filled with it. Humans used fire for everything—safety from wild animals, heat to keep warm, a means to cook their food. She'd learned to endure its presence when she'd lived here millennia ago. But that was before the Forest of Nightmares.

Another shudder tore through her. At this moment, there was no fire. Nothing at all but the two people who'd come through the gate from Esria with her. The pair who'd captured her. Freed her. A human male and the female slave he'd nearly traded Ilaria for.

Only minutes ago, the human had carried Ilaria from the clearing in which she'd lived with her guards for three centuries, into that vile forest, then through the newly opened gate to the human realm. A gate she herself had long ago sealed.

If the gate hadn't been located so close to the prison, she'd never have made it. She was certain her mind would never survive the journey through the nightmares for any length of time again.

It had taken her years to recover the first time.

She glanced at the pair kissing passionately only a few yards away. The slave, a Marceillian priestess, was still dressed in the lavender ceremonial gown that must have once belonged to her ancestors. The Marceils, the slave race of Esria, resembled the humans with their dark hair and tanned skin, though the Marceils were quite a bit shorter. This one had somehow become unenslaved until one of Ilaria's guards caught her, shearing her hair from her head and stealing the power she'd raised against them.

The human had surprised them all, refusing to leave the little slave behind.

Interesting, but of little import. Of far more importance was that at last she was free to pursue revenge and retribution against the one who'd imprisoned her, the one who'd ordered her mother's death then set himself upon the throne in the queen's place. The vile, dangerous Caller, King Rith—the only man in Esria capable of calling the dark power for which the stones of Orisis had been created, and enslaving not only the human realm, but Esria as well.

Never had she known a more dangerous man. If only her mother had seen the truth behind that smile. If only the queen had heeded Ilaria's warning. She lifted her chilled face, her gaze turning to the vastness of the human heavens and the million points of light. Fifteen hundred years had passed since she'd lifted her arms to the human sky and called down the magic to seal eleven of the twelve gates between the worlds, leaving behind not only the six evil green stones of Orisis, but also the blue draggon stone, the source of much of the queen's power and the key that opened all the gates. Unable to seal them all, she'd obscured that final gate, one deep in the Banished Lands, hoping no Esri would ever find it. For fifteen centuries, none had until the Esri, Baleris, found his way through. A few months later, the draggon stone passed through the gate, only for a few minutes, but it was enough. The draggon stone was the key that unlocked all the gates. Now all twelve were open and she had no doubt King Rith had sent men to search for the stones.

Stopping him would be difficult, if not impossible, for she'd left the stones with a human. Now, fifteen centuries later, they could be anywhere in this vast world. She had to get her hands on them before Rith did if she wanted any chance of thwarting him. Which meant she must escape her captors.

Ilaria glanced again at the couple. The kissing had ended, but they remained huddled together, soft words catching on the chill breeze. Words of love and commitment. She ought to be surprised, perhaps, that a human would fall so completely for a Marceil. Humans tended to fear anything or anyone different than themselves.

Then again, she'd taken the measure of this particular slave and found her to be a woman of uncommon courage. The man clearly recognized that. Perhaps he was without the fears and prejudices of so many of his race. Perhaps, in fifteen centuries, the humans had changed.

Regardless, the pair were wasting time.

"Why did you capture me?" Ilaria asked loudly.

The male looked up, tucking the Marceil against his side. "We *rescued* you, Princess." With a soft oath, he reached beneath his tunic and withdrew a… She didn't have a word for it. Though language came to her automatically, she needed to touch a human, a non-Sitheen, to learn all the things humans knew.

Her captor touched the small gray rectangle repeatedly with his thumb, then scowled. "Phone's dead," he muttered. "The battery was designed to last, which means the magic probably fried it."

He took the Marceil by the hand as he met Ilaria's gaze. "Let's get moving and I'll explain as we walk. If we don't find shelter soon, we're going to freeze to death." He grunted. "*I'm* going to freeze to death." He was the only one of the three who wasn't, from a human standpoint, immortal.

Without a second glance, the pair started off, leaving Ilaria standing in the snow. *Rescued,* he'd said. She hurried to catch up. "Why did you rescue me?" she demanded.

The man glanced back at her. "Were you the one who sealed the gates?"

She could deny it, but the very fact that he'd gone to such lengths to free her made it clear he already knew the answer.

"You wish me to seal them again?"

He nodded. "We have the seven stones."

She nearly stumbled with surprise. They had them all, the six stones of Orisis and her own draggon stone. Astonishing, considering the number of human lifetimes that had passed. Hope bloomed within her. Stopping Rith might not be so difficult after all.

"You'll return the stones to me, of course."

He met her gaze, something hard entering his eyes. "We need your help, Princess, but you'll forgive us if we have a hard time trusting the Esri. Any Esri. When we're certain you mean to seal the gates, we'll let you have the stones to do it. Until then, they'll remain hidden."

Her jaw compressed, anger sparking inside her. The only reason the humans had the stones was because she'd given them to them. They were hers, not theirs.

But the gleam of steel she glimpsed in the

man's eyes told her that no show of temper was likely to get her what she wanted.

Trust. She was going to have to win his trust. Which would take time she might not have.

With effort, she quieted her angry tongue. "Where are we?"

"I wish I knew. If I had to guess, I'd say northern Europe. Maybe Canada. It's damn cold, wherever it is."

"If you don't know where we are, I assume that means the stones are a distance away?"

"They're with my friends back in D.C. And the one thing I'm sure of is we're not anywhere near D.C."

"What is Dee Cee?"

"Washington, D.C. In the U.S." He glanced at her and grimaced. "Hell, you don't have any idea what I'm talking about, do you?"

"I do not."

"It doesn't matter. That's where we're going."

She could ask for nothing more. "If I'm not your prisoner, then untie me, human. Walking with my hands behind my back is tedious."

"It's Charlie, not *human,* and this is Tarrys."

His voice softened, filling with a soft wonder as he glanced at the Marceil. "My soon-to-be wife." He turned back to Ilaria, his expression hardening again. "As I'm sure you've noticed, I have a death mark or two."

"You fear I'll take your life." Esri, linked as they were, knew at once when one of their own had been killed, and by whose hand. Through the magic of their world, the killer acquired a death mark that all Esri could sense and follow. And upon which every Esri had long ago been ordered to act.

No mere human would acquire such a mark. Only a Sitheen.

"It crossed my mind," Charlie said. "It's a compulsion, isn't it? To kill those with a death mark?"

"A compulsion? No. It was a law enacted eons ago. A law I've broken more than once and have no qualms about breaking again. I don't take life unless it's absolutely necessary."

"Admirable." But the way he said the word told her he doubted her sincerity.

"Is Dee Cee where the unsealed gate came through?"

"Yes."

"How many full moons will it take us to reach it?"

A hint of amusement crinkled the corners of the human's—Charlie's—eyes. "Once I get a hold of my brother, we should be back there in a day. Two at the most."

Ilaria frowned. "How can you know that if you don't know where we are? I've been in the human realm, Charlie. I have some sense of its vastness."

"Things have changed since you were here last, Princess. With a little cash, we can get anywhere in the world in a couple of days now."

She stared at him, startled. "Humans have acquired magic."

Charlie's smile flashed white in the moonlight. "Not magic. Technology, though it may seem the same to you."

She pondered that, finding the thought exhilarating. For too long she'd been trapped in a forest glade devoid of newness, devoid of stimulation of any kind but for the conversation of the men who'd been imprisoned with her. A new and exciting human world was exactly what her mind craved.

The snow grew thicker, the walking more difficult. In the distance, the glow of light told her they'd stumbled upon other humans. And she was still tied. Her excitement turned back to annoyance. "If you want my help, human, and I believe you do or you'd not have risked the Forest of Nightmares to free me, then you must trust me. Release me from these bonds."

Charlie's gaze cut to her. "Will you help us? Will you seal all of the gates this time and leave the stones with us as you did before?"

The keen intelligence in his eyes warned her that he'd hear the lie in her words if she wasn't careful. So she answered with the truth.

"If what you say is true, I will help you." And she would, though not in the way he meant. Not in the way he wanted.

No, the gates would not be sealed this time. The stones would never again be left in human hands. She would not make that mistake twice.

Chapter 2

Harrison rested his hand on the cold roof of the police cruiser, one of a dozen cars they'd parked in the grass of Dupont Circle Park. The fire ring blazed brightly in the falling snow, lighting the huge, chalice-shaped, marble fountain it circled.

It was almost midnight.

His hand went to his head, adjusting the riot helmet Jack had procured for them on short notice. All the Sitheen were now armed with helmets and bulletproof vests, hand shields and flame throwers, like some kind of bizarre urban army straight out of a sci-fi flick. Sadly, other than the movie part, that was exactly what they were.

If he'd owned an old-fashioned suit of armor,

he'd have put it on. If the Marceils coming through that gate were half the archers Tarrys had been, the arrows would find any hole, any weakness. And Larsen's vision would still come true.

Next time, if there *was* a next time, they were meeting the invasion with complete head-to-toe body armor.

He prayed they got another chance. What if they didn't? What if they all died tonight? Who would be left to fight this war? Odds were, there were other Sitheen scattered around the world, but would they figure out what was going on before it was too late? Would they be able to stop the invasion when he and his friends had failed, or would the Esri hunt them down, one after another, and kill them before they ever had a chance?

A cold fist closed around his heart at the fear that his kids would meet that same fate. Sam and Stephie had been with him the first time he encountered an Esri. He'd taken them to see a matinee of *The Lion King* at the Kennedy Center then watched in horror as everyone in the theater turned into a zombie and started toward them as if to tear them limb from limb. All three of them would have died that day, he knew that now, if Larsen hadn't foreseen their deaths and come to warn them. If not for hers and Jack's intervention, they would have died.

He'd told Gwen, his ex-wife, to get the kids out of D.C. and keep them there until this was over. He was pretty sure she'd taken them and gone to stay with one of her cousins in Pennsylvania, but he'd told her not to tell him. There was no telling what an Esri could do and it was safer for the kids if he didn't know.

But he called every couple of days to make sure they were all right, never losing hope that Stephie would recover from whatever that Esri bastard, Baleris, had done to her.

They had to win tonight. Who would protect his kids if they failed?

Six Sitheen and Kade circled the fountain, waiting for the night's coming invasion. Jack had convinced Larsen to wait in the car, out of harm's way, with Kade's human soon-to-be wife, Autumn, and the retirees of the group, Aunt Myrtle and Norm. Norm had joined them only recently. A Sitheen and retired firefighter, he'd been the one to oversee the fire ring tonight.

Larsen had argued vehemently to be part of the fight, but though she was a warrior at heart, her battleground of training had been the courtroom. Harrison grunted. He'd never been a soldier himself, but he'd always been an athlete and he was a damned sight stronger than the Esri. In the past months, he'd procured the services of a fight coach to teach him the finer points of hand-to-hand combat. And that's exactly what this was likely to come down to. Unless the arrows hit their mark.

Or unless fate finally smiled on them and the fire circle worked. The plan was simple. The only way to kill an Esri was to set him on fire and sing the death chant. At the first sign of invasion, the Sitheen would start chanting. If any of the Esri tried to breach the wall of flame, they'd die.

In all probability, they wouldn't be so foolish, resulting in a standoff, the best possible scenario. This might be war, but they'd learned from Kade and a couple of others that not all Esri meant the humans harm. If they could keep them on their own side of the gate, all the better. If not, they'd try to capture them. If that failed, they'd do whatever they must to stop them.

They had no choice. The freedom of the entire human race was at stake.

He took another look around, satisfied that all the non-Sitheen cops and firefighters had pushed back to the other side of the street circling the park. Even though they wore bands of holly— a natural protection against enchantment— they were potentially vulnerable to Esri control. Nearby roads had all been closed. Harrison had to wonder what the locals thought was going on. The cops, too, for that matter. Only a handful at the top knew the truth. The last thing anyone wanted was panic.

The rhythmic tone of his cell phone startled him, sending his heart into a quick pound. A glance at the number told him nothing, except it wasn't his brother's phone. He swallowed back his disappointment, hesitated, then answered.

"Hello?"

"Hey, big bro. Mission accomplished."

"Charlie." Harrison closed his eyes, tipping his head back. *Thank you, God.* "It's Charlie!" he yelled.

He wasn't the only one who'd been praying for this phone call. A chorus of cheers erupted around the circle.

"Where are you?"

"Iceland."

"Iceland. Did you get the princess?"

"Of course. I'll fill you in when you get here. Fly to Reykjavik and call this number and I'll tell you where to meet us."

"What about Tarrys?"

"She's with me. I could knock your front teeth out for letting her come, but I won't. I never would have made it without her."

"I didn't *let* her come. She was going with or without my consent. She just wanted to make sure someone knew she wasn't coming right back."

"Well, she's with me permanently now." A soft note that Harrison didn't think he'd ever heard before entered his brother's voice. "She just agreed to be my wife."

Harrison's jaw dropped.

"'Congratulations' would be the appropriate response," Charlie drawled after the silence stretched too long.

"Right." Hell. "It's nearly midnight and we've got the gate circled in fire. Call me back in a couple of hours and I'll let you know when I'll be there." He cleared his throat. "Charlie… Larsen had a vision about the gate tonight. If you don't hear from me, you'll have to find your own way back."

Silence. "You're doing something different, I hope, to change the outcome?"

"Of course. But we won't know if it's enough until it's over. Glad you're back, brother."

"Be careful, Harrison." Charlie's triumphant tone had turned worried. He was the only true soldier of the group, and Harrison knew it must be killing him to be too far away to help with this fight. "I'll wait for your call."

Harrison hung up the phone.

"Did he get the princess?" Jack called.

"He did." And he thought he was marrying Tarrys. No way in hell. Tarrys was cute enough, in a little-to-no-hair kind of way. But she *wasn't human.* Not to mention the fact that Charlie had never paid her any real attention even though Tarrys had been obviously smitten with him from the start. Just how badly had she enchanted him? And Charlie had damn well better be enchanted, because if he thought he was bringing an immortal into the family…

Dammit. Harrison shoved the phone back in his pocket. All he wanted was his world back to normal. Was that too much to ask? An immortal sister-in-law was *not* the way to accomplish that.

"Where are they?" Jack asked.

"Iceland. He has Tarrys with him, too."

"It's about time something went right."

"So, what's the deal with Larsen's vision?" one of the new recruits called. "I thought the Esri were coming early."

Harrison stilled, his gaze slamming into Jack's. "When Larsen said there was no fire…"

"We assumed…" Jack grimaced. "It's almost midnight."

Ah, hell.

As if on cue, the fire went out as if it had never

been. No, they weren't coming early, they just had someone who could put out the fire.

"Call Norm," one of the recruits called.

"Esri!" another yelled.

Chaos erupted as dark forms leaped from the fountain. Harrison's pulse began to pound as a dozen short archers in gray slaves' robes began firing arrows in every direction. Marceils. Just as Larsen had foreseen.

"Stay down!" Jack's voice rang over the park.

Harrison ducked behind the car he was using as a shield. Moments later, the taller Esri began to leap out of the gate dressed in dark hooded cloaks that all but hid their extreme paleness. The Sitheen had hoped the fire would turn the invasion into a standoff. Now it was clear they were in for a full-scale battle.

Gunshots rang through the park as a couple of the humans attempted to take down the Marceils. The immortal slaves wouldn't stay down, but a gunshot seemed to take minutes for them to heal, rather than seconds, as it did the Esri.

Arrows clacked and thudded against car windows as if the Marceil didn't realize they wouldn't go through. And why should they? They didn't have cars in Esria. Harrison doubted they even had glass.

Esri leaped out of the fountain, one after another, taking off at a dead run into the night. Harrison grabbed his flamethrower and shield and ran for the nearest invader. Hiding from the arrows might be the smartest move, but if he wanted to save his world, hiding wasn't an option.

The plan was to set as many of the bastards on fire as they could. Fire wouldn't kill them unless someone sang the death chant, but it should immobilize them for a good fifteen minutes or more. Long enough to hog-tie them and pull them into a waiting refrigerator truck tricked out with layers of iron and holly to dampen their magic. Hopefully. What they'd do with them after that, they'd yet to decide, but they'd prefer to take them prisoner rather than kill them outright, if possible.

Harrison ran for an Esri fleeing in his direction as arrows whizzed by him. One arrow struck Harrison in the helmet, another hit his shield, but neither slowed him down. It was clear these archers' abilities were a far cry from Tarrys's. Either that or they fought the compulsion to fire upon the humans. Unlike humans, an enslaved Marceil maintained full awareness of what he was being forced to do. Most, he suspected, had no desire to kill them.

He cut off the fleeing Esri and fired the flame-thrower. Like magic, fire instantly engulfed the cloaked invader, his white-as-snow face taking on a mask of pain and fear. No doubt he expected to hear the death chant and explode into a million lights.

"Today's your lucky day," Harrison muttered, and left him for the hog-tying crew.

One down.

He saw another catch fire across the park. And another.

"Protect Jack!" Kade's deep voice carried to him.

Harrison saw the problem at once. Eight Esri weren't fleeing. Instead, they were going after Kade and Jack, the two with the death marks.

The humans might be trying to avoid killing

the invaders. The Esri weren't about to return the favor.

Kade ran for the Esri surrounding Jack, grabbing them, one at a time, and flinging them forty or fifty feet, as if they weighed nothing. Two recruits ran to set fire to the thrown Esri before they got up again. But though Kade fought to keep them away from Jack, the Esri weren't stupid. When Kade's hands were full flinging one of their hapless comrades, others raced past him, avoiding the giant half-blood until three had Jack surrounded. Jack fought back, his flamethrower engaged, but while he might set one or two of the bastards on fire before they touched him, he was unlikely to get all three.

Harrison ran for him, pulse pounding, the cold wind whipping at his face. He was almost there. Jack managed to set one of his attackers on fire, but as the Esri yelled with pain, an arrow struck Jack in the thigh. The cop went down.

Harrison and Kade reached him at the same moment, each diving for an Esri to knock him away before he could touch Jack and destroy him, each taking one to the ground. Unlike Jack and

Kade, Harrison had no death mark and was in no danger of being killed from a touch.

Harrison's Esri was big for his race, but no Esri without a healthy dose of human blood was muscular. While this one put up a halfway decent fight, his effort wasn't enough. Harrison grabbed the Bic lighter out of his pocket, flicked it and shoved the flame into the bastard's neck. As he leaped up and back, the Esri burst into flame.

"Harrison."

Jack's voice, tight with pain and something else, had him whirling around.

The other Esri who'd been trying to reach Jack was encased in fire. But so, too, was Kade. If anyone whispered the death chant, all those trapped in flame would die instantly.

Kade's face was a mask of pain even though the fire that encased him was different than the others, sparkling unnaturally. Mystic fire. But like the other, it had him trapped but good.

"The Esri…" Kade groaned. "One of the ones who got away. Was King Rith. I recognized him…too late. He's going after the stones."

Hell. But they had a bigger problem at the moment. Keeping Kade alive.

A quick look around told Harrison the only Esri still nearby were those encased in flame. "Tell me what to do, Kade."

"Don't sing the death chant."

Harrison grunted. Who knew Esri had a sense of humor? "I figured as much. Something a little more helpful?"

"The mystic fire will go out on its own in a couple of hours if no one activates it. But any Esri can find me. They can find any of us with death marks. They'll be hunting us."

"Then we've got to get you out of here." Harrison started barking out orders to the nearby Sitheen. "Get Myrtle, Larsen and Autumn." Myrtle was an unnaturally gifted healer and Jack needed her. And both Jack and Kade needed their women right now. "Brad, get the police van over here and six cops. Strong ones."

They might tie and drag the other Esri into a waiting truck, but Kade was one of their own now.

"How many did we catch?" Jack asked.

"Ten or eleven," Harrison replied. "But just as many escaped."

"Hell."

Larsen and Autumn ran toward them, Aunt Myrtle following at a far slower pace.

Autumn stared in horror at Kade. "You're going to die."

"Not if we have anything to say about it," Harrison said behind her. "We're going to load him into a closed police van and drive him out of the city until the flame dissipates."

The redhead's gaze swung to Harrison. "I'm going with him."

"We're both going with him." If the Esri followed, they'd be in for another fight.

Autumn stepped closer to Kade, her eyes throbbing with misery. "Can I touch you? Will I catch fire?"

Kade's expression eased. "Mystic fire can't hurt you. It's meant only for me."

"Will my touch hurt you more?"

"Never."

Without a moment's hesitation, Autumn stepped into those sparkling flames and slid her arms around Kade's waist, laying her head on his shoulder. Harrison shook his head with disbelief at the absolute trust such a move took. Trust in an *Esri*.

As the police van drove into the park, Harrison stepped forward and took charge. It took all six cops to lift the flaming seven-foot male, but they got him into the van and laid him on the floor. The cops climbed out and Autumn hopped in. She lay beside her fiancé, her arms slipping around his waist, her head on his shoulder, though he had no freedom of movement to hold her in return.

Harrison watched as she lifted her head and kissed Kade. How could she love one of those creatures? Though, admittedly, Kade was half human and didn't look Esri at all.

He closed the door on the pair and joined the driver, one of Jack's friends on the metropolitan police force. As they headed north on Connecticut, he pulled out his cell phone and called Charlie.

"We're still here, little brother."

Silence, then a loud exhale of air. "Thank God."

"Tell me you didn't acquire a death mark in Esria."

Charlie was silent for the space of two heart-beats. "Can't do that."

Dammit. He told him about Kade, then promised to get to Iceland as soon as he could. "Whatever you do, do *not* let the princess touch you."

At every turn, the Esri proved themselves to be more and more dangerous. As if it weren't bad enough the Sitheen were mortals, with all their human frailties. Now half their team had death marks. All the Esri had to do was touch them and wish them dead and they would be.

Except him.

With a slam of understanding, he realized what had to happen. Someone had to watch and guard Princess Ilaria until the next full moon. Someone without a death mark.

Him.

Ah, hell.

Chapter 3

The sun was low on the horizon on a crystal-clear December day when Harrison and the two Sitheen recruits who'd accompanied him arrived at the hotel in Reykjavik, Iceland. The hotel, like the city, was the definition of old-world Nordic charm.

Harrison had barely lifted his hand to rap on Charlie's door when the door swung open and his brother met him with a grin. They embraced, slapping one another on the back.

"Ye of little faith," Charlie chided, pulling away. "You were sure I wouldn't make it."

Harrison didn't deny it. "I'm glad I was wrong, little brother."

A flash of green across the room caught his

eye, drawing his gaze. Harrison froze. On a chair beside the window, her hands tied together in her lap, sat the palest woman he'd ever seen. And, God help him, the most beautiful. *Princess Ilaria.* Goose bumps lifted on his forearms as the hair rose on the back of his neck. *Esri.*

"Easy, bro," Charlie said quietly. "Why don't you come into the room?"

She looked exactly like the painting. *Exactly.* Both her skin and hair were pale, pale, pale, but not the ultratoothpaste-white of some of the Esri. Creamy, like new ivory, startling and stunning against the shimmering emerald green of her gown.

Striking.

Her hair fell in soft curls, framing a face that might have been considered delicate on another woman. But he sensed nothing delicate about this one. Her full, sculpted mouth sat firm upon an oval face framed by a strong, finely curved jaw. Her eyes, as brilliantly emerald as her gown, flashed with intelligence and steel, reminding him she was no twentysomething-year-old, no matter what she looked like.

Charlie thrust out his hand to the two Sitheen recruits, who were still standing in the hallway. "Charlie Rand."

"Brad Parsons," the kid replied. Not such a kid, really. Not at twenty-five. Kade had found him at Quantico, training to be a U.S. Marine.

Harrison's gaze dipped, drawn against his will to that shimmering green gown that covered the princess neck to wrists to ankles, yet hugged her form, setting off her full breasts to perfect advantage. A charge of raw attraction bolted through his blood, horrifying him. She was *Esri*. But God help him, he couldn't tear his gaze away.

"Tom Drummond," their pilot said behind him as the introductions continued without him. Tom was mid-forties, an air force colonel Kade had found who was bored and restless at a desk job in the Pentagon. All Kade had to do was touch a human to know if he or she was Sitheen. All he had to do to convince them his story was true was cut himself and let them watch him heal in an instant.

A top-notch recruiter.

Like the others, Tom had taken temporary leave

until they got this invasion under control. The President of the United States himself now knew the situation and had given them carte blanche to deal with it. Only a handful outside the Sitheen circle knew what was really going on. And they intended to keep it that way.

Struggling against his unholy fascination, Harrison finally managed to wrench his gaze from Princess Ilaria. Glancing around, he took in the clean, sparse lines of the Nordic décor before noticing Tarrys standing by the foot of the bed. She gave him a small smile unlike any he'd seen on her before. Not shy this time. Not subservient. A smile of welcome. And confidence.

She'd changed. Gone was the slave's robe, as well as the hair that had started to grow on her head. She was dressed in leather boots, dark slacks and a thick wool sweater that nevertheless accentuated her slenderness. The picture of casual bald chic. But the differences went deeper. Gone was the skittish little slave. In her place stood a woman of bearing and confidence. A woman who held herself with pride, meeting his gaze with strength and certainty.

Transformed.

Just what had happened to her and his brother in that place? He had no idea, but it occurred to him that maybe Charlie's falling for her wasn't magic after all. At least not the unnatural kind.

Charlie ushered them into the room and closed the door, then went to Tarrys, his gaze softening with an expression Harrison had never seen in his brother's eyes. Adoration. *Love.* A look utterly returned by the petite Marceil. A soft, lovely smile wreathed Tarrys's pretty face as she took the hand he proffered.

Harrison was the first to admit that he was no expert on enchantment, but he knew love when he saw it. At least in other people. Hell, between Jack and Larsen, and Autumn and Kade, he was choking on the stuff. And watching Charlie and Tarrys, he was all too afraid he was indeed about to gain an immortal sister-in-law.

Charlie pulled the small woman against him and turned to face them. "This is Tarrys, soon to be my wife."

"She's bald," Brad murmured behind him.

Charlie merely lifted an eyebrow. "So?"

"Sorry, sir," Brad said with quick contrition. His gaze skipped to Tarrys. "Ma'am. I didn't mean any offense."

Tarrys's eyes turned soft with understanding. "Few women of your world go without hair. Fewer still, willingly. It's unusual."

"Yes, ma'am, it is," Brad said. "Still, I should have kept the thought to myself."

"Neither of the women are human?" Tom asked. Harrison had briefed the men about Ilaria, but not Tarrys.

Charlie's gaze sharpened, but his voice remained even. "Both are from Esria. Both are immortal. Tarrys is a Marceillian priestess who's been enslaved by the Esri."

"And I am Princess Ilaria, the rightful queen of Esria." Ilaria's firm yet melodious voice filled the room. It was a voice that pleasured Harrison's ears and sent a thrill skating over his skin, raising goose bumps.

He frowned at his unwarranted reaction to her voice. Was she employing some kind of royal enchantment on them? But as he glanced at the others, he saw curiosity in their eyes, perhaps even awe. But not attraction. Not one looked like he felt as if his lungs were being squeezed from the inside out.

Her words echoed in the room, ringing with conviction and truth, yet somehow lacking arrogance. She was their prisoner, yet her green eyes revealed no fear. Instead, cunning and intelligence sparkled in those extraordinary eyes. Perhaps even a hint of humor. Was she laughing at them? Were they fools to believe they could capture a rattler and turn it against their enemies without getting struck themselves?

Her wide, well-shaped mouth curled ever so slightly upward as if a smile were indeed about to bloom on her face, and he watched with an anticipation that had chills of another kind sliding over his flesh. His reaction to her wasn't right, it wasn't natural.

Her otherness, her *Esri*-ness, should have repelled him. He knew that.

Yet from the moment he'd set eyes on her, he hadn't been able to turn away.

Dammit.

He clapped his hands together, desperate to

break the spell, shifting the attention back to him. "Let's get going. D.C.'s crawling with Esri and we need to get back."

Charlie made a move toward the princess. Harrison's heart plummeted to his stomach as he remembered the way Kade had gone up in flames at a single touch. Harrison lunged forward. "I've got her, Charlie."

His brother glanced at him, his eyebrow arcing. "She's tied to the chair."

"Then I'll be the one to untie her. I don't have a death mark." He didn't get his brother back only to lose him again, not like that.

Charlie shrugged. "She's all yours."

Harrison pushed past his brother and Tarrys. The princess, sitting with her back ramrod straight on the chair, watched him draw near, snagging his gaze—not gently, not kindly. Her eyes, as brilliant as the finest emeralds, bore into his, warning of battle even as they whispered of laughter. And shimmered with heat.

She'd no doubt noticed him staring at her. He steeled himself against this unholy fascination, but as he bent over her shoulder to untie the knot that held her firmly to the chair, the scent of her hair rushed his senses, slamming him with raw desire. She smelled at once exotic and sweet, like gardenias in a tropical garden. The scent drugged him. *Intoxicated* him.

Hell.

His fingers fumbled with the rope, finally freeing the knot. When he pushed back, straightening, he found her watching him with eyes warm and electric, as if she could feel the hammering of his pulse. As if hers pounded as well.

He tried to look away and failed, mesmerized by her high cheekbones and the perfect shape of her nose. By the curve of her jaw and that lush, ripe mouth that lifted at the corners ever so slightly. Even her skin enthralled him and his fingers itched to know if the pale marble perfection could possibly feel as warm and silken soft as it appeared.

As the blood pounded through his body, his mind recoiled at the turn of his thoughts. She was casting some kind of enchantment over him. There was no other explanation. With more roughness than he'd intended, he grabbed her arm and pulled her to her feet, her hands still tied in front of her.

"Let's go, Princess."

"No." To his surprise, she fought him, digging in her heels. That touch of humor had vanished, her eyes snapping with pride and anger. "Free me entirely, human. I'm tired of being bound."

He met those brilliant eyes, for a moment stumbling into their green depths before he found his footing and steeled himself with his own anger.

"As long as you're near anyone with a death mark, you're staying tied."

"I'm not a fool. I'm not going to harm my allies. Charlie is my way to the stones."

"He was. Now we all are. I'm thinking you might consider him expendable."

"And what would you do if I killed him here and now?" Her words cut as she lifted her chin and stared at him.

Ignoring the unfortunate attraction still pounding through his veins, he tightened his grip on her arm, yanking her around until he was fully in her face. "If you harm my brother in any way, the gates be damned. *I'll kill you.*"

She nodded calmly. "Which is why I would be a fool to try to harm him. I don't care that he has a death mark." One blond eyebrow rose. "I might even be inclined to forgive the mark once I have my stones."

He stilled. "You can remove death marks?"

"I can, as the rightful queen."

"Then do it."

"I need the draggon stone."

He grunted and turned, dragging her with him toward the door. "Convenient, Princess."

"You believe I'm lying? The draggon stone answers to royal blood and always has. Within it lies my power."

"You haven't had the draggon stone in fifteen centuries. Forgive me for having a hard time believing you'd have left the source of your power with us, where not even your queen could find it."

She didn't answer for a moment and when she did her voice was low and subdued. "I did what I had to do."

He glanced at her, trying to figure her out...trying to ignore her feminine assault on his senses. "So when we get you back to D.C., if we allow you to touch the draggon stone, you can forgive all the death marks?"

"If you *allow* me to touch the stone? The stone is mine, human. As the rightful queen, they're all mine."

"That wasn't my question."

Temper flared in her eyes. "Yes, I can forgive the death marks."

"Will you?"

She looked up at him, the light of challenge quickly eclipsing the anger in her eyes. Slowly, her mouth began to curl upward in an intriguing shadow of a smile that charged the already electric air between them.

"Allies help one another," she purred. "Perhaps you should be trying to convince me you're my ally, and not my enemy. Free me."

"You ask too much, Princess. I don't trust any Esri." Especially one powerful enough to weave a sensual spell over a Sitheen, for that was exactly what she had to be doing. There was no way he'd be attracted to an Esri otherwise. Not when he knew the evil they were capable of. Not when his own daughter suffered still. But despite everything logical and right, he was definitely, horrifyingly attracted to this woman.

Ilaria clenched her jaw tight as the human propelled her down the hotel's hallway. She was infuriated that he insisted on keeping her tied like a common slave. Never had humans treated her so poorly. In the old days, they'd revered her. Then again, these were no ordinary humans. They were Sitheen. Humans with a trace of Esri blood who could be neither enchanted nor tricked with glamour.

Worse, these Sitheen knew the death chant… and how to use it. Two thousand years she'd lived, yet they could destroy her in seconds.

Yes, they maddened and infuriated her, but sweet Esria, that wasn't all.

Striding beside her, tall and strong, Harrison's nearness caressed her skin with a tingling pleasure. Even through her sleeve, she felt his fingers curled around her arm, warm and fierce, yet surprisingly gentle. In the air between them, desire thickened, awareness sizzled.

When was the last time she'd felt desire like

this for a male? Not for as long as she could remember. Yet despite his sharp, distrustful eyes, there was something about this male that pulled and tugged at her in all her darkest, most vulnerable places.

He glanced at her, meeting her gaze, sending a rare force of masculine power rippling over her skin. Human males were so much more physical than Esri. So much more aggressive, more *potent*. The simple gaze of this one heated her, turning her to liquid deep inside. Passion burned in his eyes, passion walled behind a barricade of fierce control.

And anger.

For a moment, she thought she felt something more. A touch of energy. The shadow of a latent, untapped power she couldn't identify, but could feel whispering through his aura.

Strange.

He pulled her forward, his grip on her arm unyielding, and she fought him no longer, knowing too well his strength far exceeded her own. If she didn't give in, she'd find herself flung upside down over his shoulder and carried as Charlie had carried her through the gate. A princess could only take so much indignity.

Her own anger steeped and stewed even as his nearness made her blood warm and her skin dance with excitement. How was it possible he had this pull on her? If Harrison weren't human, she might question whether he possessed a rare ability to enchant an Esri. Instead, she feared the weakness was hers alone.

No, not alone. She was quite sure he shared it. And that could, possibly, work to her advantage. She must convince him that her intent was to seal the gates as they wanted her to. Convince him to hand over the stones to her. And a smitten male was so much easier to manipulate.

Of course, this human was far from smitten. He might feel desire for her, but his hatred ran deep. A hatred, she suspected, for all her kind. She might talk of being allies but they weren't and they both knew it. The humans had made it clear they didn't trust her, nor were they giving her any choice in what she did with the stones. Yes, this could be fun. She needed a little excitement after three hundred years of incarceration.

Her own special means of retribution for this human's disrespectful treatment of her.

A small smile curved her mouth at the prospect of the sensual battle to come as he led her through the room and out the door into the hallway where the others waited.

A battle she didn't intend to lose.

Chapter 4

"What are those?" Ilaria asked, nodding toward the headphones Tarrys had slipped over her ears in the private jet. "If you'd untie me and allow me to touch a human, a non-Sitheen, I would know these things."

"Headphones. And you're not touching anyone." Harrison knew that a full-blooded Esri could absorb a human's entire store of knowledge with a single touch. They might come into this world clueless, but they didn't stay that way long. Harrison sighed. "I suppose you want to watch the movie, too?"

"Of course. What's a movie?"

From the moment he'd steered the princess out of the hotel room, Harrison had become her keeper. And he was pretty certain she was enjoying driving him slowly insane. All he wanted to do was get as far from her as possible, to break this ungodly attraction that refused to die. Instead, he was stuck with her.

He grabbed another set of headphones and lifted them onto her delicate head, pushing aside the pale, curly hair covering her ears. The soft, springy feel caressed his hands and he was slammed with a longing to wrap one thick lock around his fingers and draw it to his nose to inhale its sweet scent. Ignoring her wasn't even a possibility. As he adjusted the earphones over her dainty ears, she watched him, those green eyes reflecting every ounce of the heat that had been building inside him since the moment he first touched her.

He tore his gaze from hers, refusing to fall into that sensual pit again, but her mouth moved, catching his attention, and he watched her pink tongue dart out to lick ripe, gorgeous lips. Lust sent the blood pounding through his body. With a growl, he flicked on the headset.

As sound filled the headphones, Ilaria's eyes widened, and her gaze flew to his for one startled moment before a look of pure delight crossed her face. The smile that bloomed in its wake took his breath away.

Ilaria turned away to face the small flatscreen television projecting out from the wall of the plane, breaking the spell. Harrison sat back in his seat beside her, his breathing erratic, his runaway pulse pounding in his ears. Looking up, he found his brother watching him with amusement and silent speculation.

"Go to hell," Harrison muttered. He glanced at his watch.

"When was the last time you heard from Jack?" Charlie asked.

"Right before we picked you up. He or Kade should be calling with another report within the hour."

The humor left Charlie's eyes. They were dealing with a major invasion this time, and the greatest threat the world had ever known. If King Rith got those stones, it was all over.

"Anyway..." Charlie cleared his throat and resumed his story, giving Harrison the short version of his trip through Esria. "We reached the Forest of Nightmares not a moment too soon, but Jesus, Harrison. That place will steal your mind. The name couldn't be more accurate. Whatever you're most afraid of appears. It may not be real, but damn if you don't think it is. I found myself surrounded by Esri who weren't there, and nearly run down by an eighteen-wheeler. In the forest."

Musical laughter trilled beside Harrison. Ilaria's laughter. The sound caressed his senses, stroking him inside and out. He struggled to ignore her and failed, unable to forget what Charlie had told him earlier, that she'd been incarcerated in a village no bigger than a football field. For three hundred years. No wonder she couldn't quite contain her smiles or laughter. She must be ecstatic to be free.

Even though they were essentially holding her captive.

His gaze slid to her, lingering on the creamy pale flesh of her cheek and the long expanse of silken neck peeking out through the soft cascade of curls. He breathed in her scent, sweet gardenias, and felt things tighten low in his body as his gaze dipped lower, to the ripe swell of breasts beneath that amazing gown.

"So fill me in on what's happened while we were gone," Charlie said, drawing Harrison's attention back to where it belonged—anywhere but Ilaria. A keen speculation lit Charlie's eyes. Harrison pretended not to notice.

"We're all but certain Esri came through some of the other gates last month. Reports of sexual assaults and abductions have skyrocketed in five very specific locations, all in northern Europe. London, Copenhagen and small towns in close proximity to three stone circles, one each in England, Scotland and France."

"You think the circles were originally erected as an attempt to defend against the monthly Esri invasions?"

"Seems likely, doesn't it?"

"Yeah, it does. So, tell me about the Sitheen recruits."

"Kade's been traveling almost constantly, from

one military base to another, and from police station to police station. Once we've exhausted the most likely places to find trained warriors, he'll expand the search."

"How many has he found?"

"Six. We lost one last night during the battle. One of the Marceils' arrows went right through his eye."

"Damn. So who do we have other than Brad and Tom? Handy that Tom's a pilot, by the way."

"It is." Tom was flying the jet, Brad keeping him company. "Norm is a retired firefighter in his seventies. He and Myrtle hit it off as if they were made for one another."

Charlie smiled. "A bit of romance?"

"No doubt about it. The other two are brother and sister. Paige is a detective with the Richmond police, mid-forties, and a crack shot. Frank is her brother, also a cop, though not as fit. Still, he knows what to do in a fight."

"Who did we lose?"

"A young navy ensign. The most promising of the bunch."

Charlie swore softly. "Myrtle couldn't help him?"

"The arrow punctured his brain. He was killed instantly. Myrtle's a gifted healer, but she can't raise the dead."

Harrison went on to fill his brother in on the full battle, struggling to forget the woman who sat beside him, which turned out to be an impossible task. Her presence filled the air.

He and Charlie were still talking an hour and a half later when the movie finally finished. Tarrys pulled off her headphones and stood up. "I need to move around."

Charlie watched her, the look in his eyes all predatory male. "I'll go with you." He rose and looped his arm across Tarrys's shoulder, the air crackling between them. "Maybe we can find something to eat."

Harrison grunted. If it was food on Charlie's mind, Harrison was a chimpanzee. More likely, his brother was planning to join the mile-high club. If he hadn't already.

As the pair walked off together, Harrison

turned to find Ilaria watching them with a speculative and knowing gaze of her own.

"Do you want the headphones off?" he asked her.

That gaze turned to him, heat swirling in the depths of her eyes. "For now."

His pulse began to speed even before he reached for her. If only he could assign the task to someone else. Bracing himself, he lifted his hands and took hold of the headphones, that soft-as-silk hair of hers teasing and caressing his sensitive flesh as he pulled them away.

Her gaze never left his, her eyes hot as sin as her tongue slowly licked her lips. "They've gone to find a place to mate in privacy. It's the first chance they've had since we came through the gate."

"You don't know that. They may be looking for food."

One pale eyebrow rose, hot laughter dancing in her eyes. "Are you truly so naive?"

Harrison scowled. "No." He sat back in his seat, his eyes still caught in hers. His gaze turned rueful. "I'm sure they're doing it, too."

Answering humor flickered in eyes that steamed even as they danced with mischief. "I'm attracted to you, human. More than I've been to any male in a long, long time. While your brother mates with the Marceil, let me take you inside my body."

Her words all but blew away his rigid control, a glorious picture erupting in his head of him pulling her gown up to her waist, freeing himself, then pulling her down to straddle him as he pushed deep, deep inside her heat. Blood throbbed in his veins, beating a carnal pulse as he grew harder and harder and harder.

"I'm not having sex with you." His words were little more than a growl, his voice choked with desire.

Her eyes dimmed. Not enough that anyone else would probably have noticed, but he did.

"Because I'm Esri." It wasn't a question.

"Yes."

She looked away, stealing the heat of her gaze. "That's too bad, human. You would have found pleasure with me. We both would have."

Begging his body to settle down, he sat back in his seat. "The name is Harrison. Not 'human.'"

She watched him. "You're not like the others, Harrison. You have a power they lack. A power unnatural to humans."

His heart gave an awkward thud. "What do you mean?"

In her expression he saw absolute seriousness for once. When she spoke, the seductive tone was missing. "I don't know. It's unlike anything I've ever felt. Familiar, yet not, and deep within you. Nothing that's ever risen to the surface. Perhaps nothing you'll ever be able to reach."

As badly as he wanted to tune out her words, he couldn't. *Because he already knew.*

Most of the Sitheen had discovered strange gifts that had apparently been passed down to them from their Esri ancestors. Larsen's premonitions of death, Jack's ability to talk to his ancestors, Myrtle's healing ability. Neither he nor Charlie had appeared to have any Esri gifts. Until he'd touched the draggon stone and felt a strange thrill of recognition, as if the power in the stone had welcomed him. He'd only touched it once, as he had the other six stones. The latter had sent an unpleasant crawling sensation climbing into his head from the base of his skull.

Both times, he'd asked Charlie if he felt anything. Both times Charlie had denied it. Harrison preferred to think whatever he'd felt was just his imagination, but he'd never really believed it. And he'd never stopped wondering what it meant.

The princess's assertion that there was something strange going on inside him just confirmed his own suspicion. And he couldn't decide if that was a good thing or bad. While he wanted nothing to do with Esria, he'd be a fool to ignore anything that might help them win this war.

The question was could he trust a word the princess said? He just didn't know.

Her gaze dropped to his lap, to the erection that still strained painfully against his zipper. "Let me touch you, Harrison," she said, her voice low and husky. "Let me feel your power."

"Yeah, right." He grabbed the headphones and pushed them back over her ears with minimal care. "Watch another movie," he said gruffly, punching the play button. He rose and moved to the other side of the plane and sat down where he could keep an eye on her, but not close enough to be tempted.

His hands curled around the seat arms, clenching until his knuckles turned white at the thought of her touching him. At the thought of her straddling him…

He groaned from the pulsing ache of need and forced his gaze out the window to the sea of sunlit clouds. Anywhere but on her.

He wasn't sure how long he'd sat there, trying to catch his breath and still the racing beat of his heart, when the onboard phone rang.

Harrison shoved himself from his seat and grabbed it.

"We've got trouble," Jack said a moment later.

"Hold on, Jack. Charlie!"

As he returned to his seat beside Ilaria, she met his gaze, her eyes sharp and serious. "Take off my headphones. I would hear this."

After a moment's indecision, he did as she asked, then sat beside her as Charlie and Tarrys joined them, both flushed with that insufferable glow. He jammed a button and held the phone on his knee.

"You're on speaker, Jack. Charlie and Tarrys are here, too."

"Glad to have you back, Charlie. Have you acquired a death mark?"

"I have."

"Then you're with us. Larsen and I were attacked by half a dozen Esri thugs a couple of hours ago. They had a singer." A singer was the term they used for an Esri who could enchant surrounding humans with a song, turning them into his own personal weapons. "We nearly didn't make it out of there. Kade's joined us and we're on the run. We're trying to come up with a way to turn the tables on them."

"So they're not going for the stones?"

"Best we can tell, they're neither organized nor heading in any particular direction. Except ours. But we don't know where King Rith is. Kade hasn't seen him since midnight, and the rest of us don't know what he looks like."

Beside him, Ilaria tensed. "King Rith is here?"

Harrison nodded. "He came through last night with a large number of guards and Marceils."

"Where are my stones?" she demanded.

"Forgive me, Princess," Jack said. "But that's not information we can share at this point. I assume Charlie told you why he rescued you?"

"You wish me to seal the gates again."

"Yes, we do. When the time comes, we'll allow you access to the stones."

She scoffed. "Sealing the gates will do neither of us any good as long as Rith and his men remain on this side. You *must* give me the stones so that I can protect them."

"Can you seal the gates other than at the full moon?" Jack asked.

"Unfortunately, no. The draggon stone, the source of my power, hasn't the ability to open the gates early. But if Rith gets his hands on the other six, the stones of Orisis, he'll be able to use their dark power to do so."

"If he gets the stones, won't he just tear down the walls between the worlds?" Charlie asked.

She shook her head. "Such powerful magic can only be called upon at the Temple of the Ancients deep in the Dark Mountains of Esria. He'll open the gates and flee, which is why you must give me the stones, and quickly. I'll not only protect them until the full moon, but I'll forgive your death marks."

"You can do that?" Jack asked, clearly surprised. "Hold on."

Harrison could hear Jack talking to someone in the background. A moment later, he was back.

"Kade confirms she should have that ability once she has the draggon stone in her possession."

"Who is Kade to know such things?" Ilaria asked, once more the imperious royal.

If only her demands made her less attractive. They didn't.

"You know him as Kaderil the Dark," Jack said.

Harrison saw her eyes flare and watched her mouth open with disbelief. "He's Esri."

"He's half Esri and he's one of us now."

Her shocked gaze met Harrison's.

Charlie leaned forward. "If King Rith has the ability to sense the stones, then the moment we bring the draggon stone out of hiding, he'll be on it. We need to leave it hidden. Besides, I'm not sure what good removing the death marks will do when we're still hunting Esri. We'll just get them back again."

"I agree," Jack said. "Our plan is to capture King Rith and the rest of his guards before the full moon."

Ilaria's graceful hands fisted in her lap. "You must kill him, not capture him. He's far too dangerous. No Caller can be allowed to live."

Jack's voice was wry. "I was trying to spare your sensibilities, Princess, but we'd come to that conclusion, as well. King Rith has to die. We'll capture whatever Esri we can, but before those gates are sealed, they'll all be back in Esria. Or dead. Leaving any on this side with the stones will defeat the purpose of sealing the gates."

"Killing is not our way, human. But under the circumstances, I agree. You did not start this war. I do not blame you for doing what you must to protect yourselves."

Harrison watched her, trying to decide if she was telling the truth or simply telling them what they wanted to hear. His gut said the former.

Then again, he wasn't sure why he should be surprised. King Rith and his goons had killed her mother and imprisoned Ilaria for three hundred years. She deserved a little revenge.

Jack continued. "Kade believes King Rith will go after Princess Ilaria if he realizes she's here. He'll try to eliminate the competition for the throne. Harrison, since you're the only one without a bull's-eye on your forehead, you'll need to get her out of harm's way until we catch him."

As he'd expected. He glanced at Ilaria as a knowing little light flickered to life in her eyes and a seductive shadow of a smile slowly lifted the corners of her mouth. Once more, the thought of her straddling him intimately roared through his head, sending his blood pressure soaring. Any hope of getting his libido back under control crashed to the ground.

From the moment he'd met her, he'd anticipated a battle. What he hadn't expected was for the battle to be sensual, or that his own body would become his worst enemy.

Chapter 5

"Would you cease with that?" Ilaria snapped, hating the quaver in her voice, but unable to control it. Beside her, as he ushered her and Tarrys through the busy Reagan National Airport, Harrison flicked the small lighter at his side on and off, on and off. A constant reminder—*a threat*—of what he'd do to her if she so much as breathed on the Marceil.

"I said I'll not touch her, and I won't." She tore her gaze from him and that awful lighter, trying to focus instead on her incredible surroundings. Above, the soaring, gilded ceiling of the airport curved sharply downward like a beautiful flower too heavy for its stem.

At least Harrison had untied her, though she

was well aware that he'd done it not as a concession to her, and certainly not because he trusted her, but to avoid the attention they'd otherwise draw in this very public place.

Even such a tiny fire had raven wings fluttering in her chest as she struggled against full panic.

The moment the plane had landed, Charlie had left, afraid his death mark would draw King Rith to them. The other two Sitheen who'd accompanied Harrison to Iceland remained, and now followed close behind.

She was frustratingly tired of being treated as a prisoner. But until she got those stones, she wouldn't escape. Even if she could.

Trying to ignore Harrison and the flame that threatened to strip her composure one flicker at a time, she studied the humans passing by. Most glanced at her, then away, as if by noticing her they might offend. In the old days, before she'd sealed the gates, humans often gaped at her, their faces either filling with terror, or awe and wonder.

She much preferred the latter, though it appeared that receiving homage from the humans was a thing of the past. Indeed, from what she'd been able to glean, the humans as a race did not remember the Esri.

A situation that was certain to change if Rith had his way.

As Harrison led them through the wide glass doors to the outside, he took hold of her upper arm, a firm grip she'd find impossible to escape, she was certain. Once more, the feel of his fingers sank through the fabric of her sleeve and into her skin, sending tendrils of warmth burrowing into her blood. Not a sweet warmth, for there was nothing kind about his touch that sought only to ensure Tarrys's safety. No, despite her frustration and wariness with the man, this heat lifted her pulse in a way that was all too pleasant. All too carnal.

Without a doubt, she desired him. As he did her. Sooner or later, she'd enjoy acting on that desire, if she could ever get him to unbend that far. A very big *if.* He wasn't a man given to impulsive action, not unless that action was in defense of his brother. Interesting that she should be so sure about that, given that she'd known him only a matter of hours. But she didn't doubt her own assessment. In a way she couldn't quite explain, she felt as if she'd known him far longer than just the day.

Keeping firm hold of her, Harrison led the small group across the paved street to where numerous vehicles sat. A *parking garage*. She knew the words, for she acquired language instantly, though it was taking her far longer to make sense of it all than it would if he'd simply let her touch a human and learn what they knew. The man was so irritatingly distrustful.

On the second level, they came to a stop behind a small, bright blue car. A series of beeps sounded, the lights flashing. As the Marceil started around the left side of the conveyance, Harrison tugged her right, pulling something from his pocket.

Ilaria glanced down, afraid he was going for the lighter again. Instead, he'd removed something metal. Her eyes widened, then narrowed with anger as she identified the manacles that now hung from his fingers.

Her eyes snapped upward as she speared him

with a sharp, stinging gaze. "You risk my ill will, human. A dangerous thing to do considering what you need of me."

"Sorry, Princess." But his tone held not the slightest edge of remorse. Instead, he pulled on her arm, snapping one loop of metal around her wrist before she could stop him.

Ilaria tried to jerk her other hand out of his reach, but he merely turned her, pushing her against the car, face-first, and snapped the second manacle around her other wrist. Only one other time in her entire life had she been treated so poorly—the morning she was hauled from her bed, accused of treachery and transported to the Forest of Nightmares.

If only she had magic that would work against a Sitheen!

She kicked back at him, but her gown hampered her movement and her heel collided with his shin with little more than a dull thud. He moved closer, pinning her against the car, pressing a hard ridge into her lower back. She stilled, taking a harsh breath, feeling his desire. Inside her, an answering need flared.

"Release me."

"Not on your life." His voice sounded close to her right ear.

Then mate with me, she wanted to say, but held her tongue, knowing she'd only anger him further.

Sliding one arm around her waist, he pulled her back against his muscular chest, the hard length of his erection nestled firmly against her. He opened the door, then slid to the right, his hand once more only around her arm.

"Get in."

She glared at him over her shoulder. "Not until you start treating me with respect."

Gripping her shoulders, he wrenched her around to face him, reminding her how much bigger he was than her. Overpowering her with his sheer maleness.

"Cooperate, Princess, and we'll get along fine." He speared her with hot, hard eyes. "Don't, and we may find you more trouble than you're worth."

A cool trickle of fear slid down her spine, but she met him glare for glare. "You won't end me. You need me."

"Do you really want to test that theory?" He let the question, heavy and disquieting, hang between them. "Get in the car, Ilaria, or I'll pull out the lighter again."

"You're a barbarian."

"No. But neither am I a fool. I'll show you the respect due your rank when and if I decide to trust you. Until then, you're the enemy."

She stared him down, refusing to bend. "You risk everything you want, human."

He didn't reply. Instead, his hand went to his pocket and that hated lighter.

With a huff of anger, Ilaria forced down her pride and slid into the low-slung automobile as he'd demanded.

Harrison followed her, leaning across her to pull yet another restraint across her chest. Desperately, she tried to ignore him, struggling against the physical appeal of the man, but his nearness filled her senses all over again. His scent was a heady mix of the strange facets of the human's modern realm—the air in the airplane, the lingering scent of some intriguing aftershave. But also of wool and wind and warm, masculine male. And she *wanted*.

"Why are you tying me down? Are you afraid I'll attack you with my teeth?"

He glanced at her, his strong face only inches away, so close she could see flecks of gold in his eyes. Heat swirled in those gray-green depths as they caught hold of hers, holding her fast. In his cheek, a muscle leaped. Between his eyebrows, a frown slowly appeared, a pair of tiny lines like the arc of bird wings.

"Believe it or not," he said softly, his voice no longer filled with anger, "the seat belts are to keep us safe in case we get into an accident."

"No accident could harm me." Her own voice was soft with breathlessness.

"Nevertheless, it's the law." Tearing his gaze away, he glanced down, fastening the belt with a metallic click. Pulling away, he straightened and closed her door, then went around the car to get in the other side. The other two Sitheen had apparently left, for only the Marceil sat in the backseat—directly behind Harrison, where Ilaria couldn't possibly touch her.

Harrison steered the vehicle into the heavy traffic, silent for a time before he glanced into the mirror, a pensive expression on his face. "Charlie tells me you're a priestess, Tarrys."

Ilaria glanced at the Marceil, watching a soft confidence fill the slave's expression. "I am, though it matters little anymore."

"You and Charlie are really getting married?"

A smile bloomed on the other woman's face with a depth of joy Ilaria had rarely seen. "He asked me to be his wife, Harrison, and there's nothing I want more."

Harrison frowned. "Why would you tie yourself to him? You're immortal. He's only got fifty or sixty years at most."

The Marceil's smile dimmed. "I'm aware of that, but I love him and will stay by his side for as long as Charlie and your God allow."

Ilaria couldn't imagine feeling that deeply for someone. For anyone. She'd had friends and companions aplenty through the years, though most she'd not seen in centuries. The men incarcerated with her within the forest for three hundred years had become closer to her than family, almost extensions of herself. Once she returned to Esria, she'd find a way to free them. But though she loved them like brothers, not a man among them had ever broken through the walls of her heart. Not a one had ever made her feel, even for a moment, a shadow of the joy she saw in the Marceil's face.

What would it be like to love another so deeply? So completely? What would it be like to be loved like that in return? Men aplenty had professed love for her over the years. Yet not a one had ever looked at her with the devotion she saw in Charlie's eyes every single time he gazed at Tarrys. In her experience, few Esri ever loved like that.

As they drove in silence, Ilaria watched out the window, fascinated and not a little awed by the sheer magnitude of the humans' dominance over their world. As in Reykjavik, buildings rose high above her head, flowing in every direction, as far as her eyes could see. There were subtle differences between the two cities—Reykjavik's buildings appeared more colorful to her untrained eye, Washington's more artistically decorative. But both were so far beyond anything she'd ever seen, as to be nearly indistinguishable.

Beside the buildings, the few people that walked were bundled beneath so many layers of hats and coats that she could barely see them. Most traveled in conveyances such as the one they rode in now. Her hand caressed the soft leather seat. A place of surprising warmth and comfort.

As Harrison stopped at an intersection, Ilaria glanced out her window to find the male in the vehicle next to them staring at her. As she met his curious gaze, he turned away.

"Do you ever use glamour?" Harrison asked.

She turned to meet his own curious gaze. "No."

"Most of your kind do."

"I'm the princess."

"What difference does that make? You're used to people staring?"

She glanced forward as the car started moving again. "In the old days, the only Esri who used glamour on the humans were those who meant them harm."

"And you didn't."

"No."

Harrison was quiet for a couple of minutes as he drove. When he once more came to a stop at a light, he glanced at her. "At one time, I assumed the Esri *always* meant humans harm, but I guess I know better than that. Kade's parents apparently lived in a village where Esri and humans lived together. Mostly mated pairs and families, from what we've gathered."

She glanced at him. "Those Esri who see humans as little more than animals either have had no contact with your kind except for the enchanted unfortunates brought into Esria as slaves, or they've never taken the time to speak to humans without enchanting them. That's not to say the other Esri treated your people well. Most still took advantage of our ability to enchant your race. But not all. There were always Esri who took it upon themselves to befriend and protect the humans. Often they were mistaken for angels."

Harrison shot her a disbelieving look. *"Angels?"*

Ilaria lifted an imperious brow. "We're not *all* the monsters you believe us to be."

He didn't answer, but his distrust hung thickly in the air.

They fell into a disquieting silence until Harrison pressed a button and music of a kind similar to what she'd heard through the headphones filled the small interior of the car. She felt as if her senses were under attack by an exciting, heady assault—the amazing sights that surrounded her, the sound of the pulse-pounding music, the rumble of the engine beneath her. And the scent of warm, intriguing male. She found herself smiling as excitement and pleasure set up a quick tattoo in her pulse. She'd always loved the new and the different, which was why she'd often visited the human realm. If not for Rith, she might stay here awhile. Perhaps a long while. But she had no time to visit, no time to explore this strange world. Not with so much at stake.

A short while later, Harrison pulled off the road and into a wide drive that curved before a tall building. As the car came to a stop, three people pushed through the front doors—two women and a man—and hurried toward them as if they'd been waiting.

Tarrys opened the car door. "Thank you, Harrison." She flew out the door, closed it with a push and rushed around the car and straight into the outstretched arms of the older of the two women. A human, Ilaria was certain, yet she greeted Tarrys as if she were a long-lost daughter.

The younger woman, an exceedingly tall female with bright orange hair, squeezed Tarrys's shoulder even as her curious gaze found Ilaria.

Harrison turned off the engine. "Wait here."

She gave him a disbelieving look. Where could she possibly go when he'd bound her hands and strapped her fast to the seat?

For one startling moment, a gleam of humor sparkled in his eyes as he met her disgruntled gaze, as if he'd read her thoughts. Then he turned away and opened his door.

"I'll be right back." He climbed out of the vehicle and joined the others, shaking hands with the older man. She couldn't hear the words shared by the small group, but over and over their gazes turned toward her with wary curiosity.

Ilaria turned away, tired of being an oddity. Tired of being the enemy. Soon enough, she'd return to Esria and receive a welcome fit for the new queen. A cautious welcome, perhaps, for none would want to antagonize Rith. But a quiet celebration was more than fine with her.

The new queen.

She caught her breath against the unexpected stab of grief. For so long she'd desired only to be free of the Forest of Nightmares and to return to the world she'd known, if not always loved. A world ruled by her mother, the queen. Only now, with her return imminent, was it beginning to sink in that the world she'd left no longer existed. Her mother was dead. And if she wasn't very, very careful, King Rith would see that she met the same fate.

Harrison drove in silence, Ilaria beside him, as he headed to Crystal City in the Northern Virginia suburbs, and home. He glanced at her as she looked out the window without seeming to see the sights that must be incredible to her. It was just after dark and the city was fully lit and at its most beautiful, yet her gaze appeared fixed on nothing.

All over again, he was struck by her beauty, her profile at once strong and delicate, those pale curls draping across her shoulders like a living shawl. Her anger at him had dissipated almost as quickly as it had risen. So different from Gwen. His ex-wife had possessed an uncanny ability to nurse a good anger until he thought she'd never let it go.

He grunted. In the end, Gwen hadn't let it go. She'd divorced him. The divorce had been his fault, he knew that. He'd never been, nor ever cared to be, the devoted, attentive husband she'd hoped for. Sometime between their wedding and Sam's birth, he'd realized whatever feelings he'd thought he had for her were gone. But he'd made a promise to stand by her and he'd intended to. And, of course, there was his son to consider and, later, his daughter.

The thought of Stephie clenched like a cold vise around his heart.

It wasn't long after Stephie was born that Gwen had decided she'd had enough. He couldn't give her what she wanted. He couldn't give anyone that much of himself. Except maybe his kids.

And now he hardly ever saw them. Especially since the arrival of the Esri.

God, but he hated those bastards. His gaze snapped to the one beside him, but that flare of hatred died as he took in her lovely, pensive face. She seemed sad to him, and for some reason that bothered him. But he thought he understood.

"You've traded one prison for another, haven't you?"

She turned to him, her face lit by the passing headlights, an unspoken question in her eyes.

"You look unhappy," he said quietly.

Turning back to the front, she tipped her head back against the seat. "I was thinking about my mother. It sounds foolish, but it's finally hit me that she won't be there when I return. I knew the moment she died. Three hundred years I've known she was gone. But I've been gone, too. In a different way, perhaps, but gone all the same."

"You haven't been out of that forest since she was killed."

"No. And in some illogical part of my mind I've always imagined she'd be there when I got home. Until tonight."

"Because the prospect of returning home is no longer a dream."

"Yes." She met his gaze again, as if surprised he understood.

Harrison nodded. "You haven't seen your world since it changed, since she left it. Not until you go back and see it for yourself will you be able to fully accept that she's gone. We call it closure."

She blinked rapidly. In the light of a streetlamp, he glimpsed a sheen of tears.

"I'm sorry, Ilaria. This has to be very hard for you."

Out of the corner of his eye, he saw her stiffen and waited for her pride to reassert itself.

To his surprise, she relaxed against the seat and sighed. "It's foolish to mourn her. We never got along."

He snorted softly. "Believe me, it doesn't matter. Parents are parents. It's a tie that never completely lets go of you, even when you want it to."

"I suppose." She lifted a hand to her forehead. "I'm concerned, too, about the reason King Rith gave my people for imprisoning me in the forest."

"You don't know?"

Dropping her hand, she turned her head, a hint of a smile lifting her lips, though no smile reached her eyes. "Unlike you, we have no form of communication except one. The guards were ordered to incarcerate me in the forest and so they did. We never heard from the outside world again."

He had trouble wrapping his mind around such a concept. Three hundred years.

"Are you afraid your people may have been turned against you?"

"Not turned against me, no. At least I hope not. But I have no illusions but that Rith will do whatever he must to keep his throne. He's always been an ambitious, power-hungry male without morals. He'll either try to capture me and send me back to the forest, or try to force someone to kill me as he did my mother. And that's if he doesn't get his stones. If he does, if he acquires the ultimate Caller's power, there will be no laws to contain him. We'll suffer as badly as you will."

Harrison's hand lifted from the steering wheel, as if to reach for her and give her shoulder a gentle squeeze of reassurance, but he forced his grip back on the wheel instead. What was he going to do, tell her everything would all work out in the end? What were the chances?

Instead, they continued through the streets of D.C. in silence.

As they crossed the bridge back into Virginia, Ilaria seemed to once more take an interest in the view outside the car. She leaned forward, looking up with awe as they passed beneath towering office buildings.

"Your world fascinates me."

"It's changed in fifteen hundred years."

"You have no idea."

"I have some idea. We were mostly goat-herders back then."

She glanced at him with a small, genuine smile before turning back to the window. "Humans were more than goat-herders. But what you've accomplished since is extraordinary. I wish I had time to fully explore the wonders of your world."

Her words were quietly said, but filled with such depth of longing that something inside him responded. For one inexplicable moment he wanted to be the one to show her, to teach her.

He tried to imagine her in a ball cap and jersey cheering beside him at a Redskins game. Or learning to water-ski on the Potomac.

The picture *that* put in his head, of the Esrian princess in her shimmering green gown on water skis, had him choking on a burst of errant laughter. But she wouldn't be in a gown, would she? She'd be in a bathing suit. A skimpy, form-hugging scrap of fabric showing far too much pale, perfect skin.

The thought intrigued him more than he would have thought possible. And that just disturbed him.

"Are you laughing?" she asked, her tone incredulous. As if he never laughed.

"No." But it occurred to him that telling her what had caused his momentary loss of control might make her feel worse than she already did. She might be the enemy, but as hard as he tried, he couldn't hate her. He couldn't even dislike her. The woman had more facets than a diamond. In the same breath she could change from a seductive siren to a playful imp, from an imperious royal to a hard-eyed warrior. And through it all, he sensed a disturbing vulnerability. A woman in danger from not one world, but two.

He'd known her how long? A matter of hours, yet he felt as if he'd known her for years. As if on some fundamental level he'd always known her. The woman confused the hell out of him. And not for the first time he wondered if she'd cast some kind of spell over him.

He drove through Crystal City and into the parking garage beneath his condo building, then parked the car and came around to release her. As he opened the door, she looked up at him with eyes as puzzled as he suspected his own were. Was she as confounded by him as he was by her?

The thought did nothing to ease his turbulent mind.

Steeling himself, he bent down to unfasten her seat belt, but her scent ambushed him, sinking into his pores, into his blood. On a primitive level, he felt the pull of her, every cell of his body wanting to move toward her, as if drawn by some invisible force.

He fought his way back into that dark room in his mind, that place of calm and control, clawing his way inside, ignoring the nearly overwhelming desire to touch her. Instead, he unfastened her seat belt, then grabbed the key to her handcuffs out of his pocket and released her before he drew unwanted attention inside. He helped her out of the car, then kept one hand tight around her upper arm as he led her to the elevator.

"You live here?" she asked. "It's big."

The elevator arrived, the doors sliding open. Three people hurried out and he ushered her inside. "I live in one small section of the building, on one of the upper floors. Many people live here."

Beneath his fingertips he could feel the heat of her skin rising through her sleeve to sink into his flesh. He released her arm and looked up, watching the floor numbers flash as he struggled to ignore her, struggled to find that calm center he'd already lost.

When the elevator stopped, he motioned her out, then led her down the hallway toward his apartment. With every step, every breath, he fought his awareness of her—the way her hair curled around her shoulders and brushed his arm, the way she moved with a fluid grace and royal dignity. The way her sweet, exotic scent wrapped around him in a warm cloud of desire.

He pulled her to a stop before his door and dug out his keys with a hand that was not quite steady as he fought to corral his raging libido. Opening the door, he stood back for her to enter, then flipped on the light switch, lighting his living room.

The condo wasn't extravagant, though it was by no means small, and he'd furnished it with good, solid furniture and leather upholstery. Three of his walls remained blank but for an uneven coat of beige paint. He kept meaning to buy prints or something, but never got around to it since most of his hours he spent at the office.

The fourth wall was covered with drawings his kids had made for him over the years. And photos of Sam and Stephie—photos he couldn't look at right now.

Closing the door behind him, he turned back to Ilaria to find her watching him with eyes devoid of seduction or cunning. Eyes that whispered of knowledge and experience he could never hope to understand, and a loneliness he understood all too well. The beauty of her face enchanted him, but it was her eyes that drew him closer, her spirit bright behind the brilliant green. The poets had gotten it wrong all those years ago. Ilaria's eyes weren't a window to her soul, but a doorway.

He didn't want this empathy toward her, this attraction. She was Esri, for heavens sake. But he saw nothing ugly inside her. No evil, no cruelty.

He stared at her, unable to turn away. Without realizing how, he found himself standing a handsbreadth in front of her. The need to touch her overwhelmed him. An ache in his chest caused him to lift his hand. His knuckles stroked her cheek, finding that pale skin every bit as warm and soft as he'd imagined. Even that barest touch sent heat flushing his skin, and need tightening deep inside him.

The need to touch her, to *taste* her, had grown steadily since the moment he'd first seen her across the hotel room in Reykjavik and wouldn't be denied a moment longer.

As one, they moved toward one another, two magnets drawn against their will. A heartbeat later, she was in his arms, his mouth covering hers, one hand sliding over her slender back, the other diving into her silken hair, cradling her delicate head as he kissed her. She swamped his senses, her taste like forbidden fruit, her scent like gardenias, the feel of her lips warm, soft and perfect.

Passion exploded, heat and desire raging through his blood. Nothing mattered but touching her, tasting her, getting inside her *in some way*. His tongue slid along the line of her lips and she opened for him, stroking him as he swept inside. A moan of pleasure cascaded from her throat, and his senses tumbled. She stroked him back, tongue against tongue, her hands curled around his neck, her fingers sliding through his hair.

She was raging passion and infinite sweetness. Need and strength, and tender warmth. And he'd been waiting for her. So long, he'd been waiting.

As he lifted his head to change the angle of the kiss, his eyes drifted open. His gaze tripped over the laughing gap-toothed image of Stephie hanging on the wall behind Ilaria. Stephie in her pink sundress, laughter on her face, love for her daddy dancing in her eyes.

He froze. An Esri had stolen that laughter, yet here he was kissing one. *Kissing* one.

The realization sliced across his mind, short-circuiting the electricity arcing through his body.

Esri. What in the hell was he thinking? What was he *doing?* He wrenched back as if she'd burned him.

Ilaria stared at him, her heavy-lidded expression stunned and confused. Her mouth was swollen and damp from his kisses, a perfect rosy pink that had his hands curling around her shoulders, his muscles straining against the nearly overwhelming need to pull her back into his arms.

"What are you doing to me?" In his mind, the words sounded accusatory, but to his ears the question only sounded confused. "You're enchanting me."

She shook her head. Her lips parting as if in denial. But even as he watched, they closed softly on a smile. A sad smile. "You don't want to desire me. But you do."

And she was right. Exactly right. He was a man

who valued control above almost anything, yet within moments of meeting her, she'd begun disassembling every ounce of control he possessed, and he'd yet to build them back. It was all he could do not to pin her to the wall and take everything she offered.

Instead, he grabbed her upper arm more tightly than necessary and steered her toward his bedroom.

"What are you doing?" she demanded softly.

"I need sleep. I'll give you the bed."

The melancholy was gone from the emerald depths of her eyes, replaced by a seductive snap. "You'll share it with me." It wasn't a question.

Harrison scowled. He already struggled for control against the sensual tornado that had laid waste to his senses, yet she acted completely composed. Acted... Was it all an act? Was she controlling him?

His fingers spasmed.

He dragged her to his bed and pulled the handcuffs out of his pocket, snapping one around her wrist.

"Harrison."

"I'm just making sure I can sleep without worrying about getting a knife in the back."

"You think I mean to stab you?"

"I'm not expecting a literal knife, necessarily. But I don't trust you. So you're staying tied. Lie down, Ilaria."

She made no move to comply, staring at him, her mouth hard. The seductress had fled, the warrior taking her place. "What if Rith tracked us here? What if we're attacked while you sleep? I'll have no means of defending myself."

"I never sleep soundly. If anyone tries to get in, I'll free you. Now lie down."

Challenge and anger glittered in her eyes, but she didn't struggle against his hold as she had in the parking garage. He was both glad and a little disappointed she'd chosen not to fight him again.

"Lie down, Ilaria."

Those green eyes hardened until they resembled the stone whose color they possessed. For a moment, he thought she intended to call his bluff, which really didn't bother him at all. Picking her up and depositing her on the bed would be no hardship. Resisting following her down might be another matter.

She stared at him for several more moments, then with a disgusted sigh, lowered herself to the bed and stretched out on her back slowly, regally. With angry eyes, she watched as he lifted her arms above her head, threaded the cuff through two spindles on his headboard, then attached the free cuff to her other wrist.

"You tread dangerously, human."

Harrison straightened and looked down at her. "I do what I have to, Princess. Now, sleep. Assuming Esri sleep. There's no telling what tomorrow will bring."

With effort, he turned away from her, grabbed the extra pillow and a blanket from the closet, and retreated to the living room. He stretched out on the sofa, but sleep was a long time coming. Not only did the passion continue to rage in his blood, but he couldn't quiet the disturbing thought that her immortal life was in his hands. And, thanks to her and her entire, miserable race, his own life was spinning out of control.

* * *

Ilaria shifted her legs on the bed, restless and bored, unable to roll over or sit up. She could barely move.

Barbarian.

It infuriated her that he treated her with so little respect. With no respect!

And what disturbed her mightily in the hours after he left her to find his sleep was that the lingering passion from his kiss still held her tight in its grip. Yes, she'd been encouraging his advances from the moment she first felt the mutual desire between them, but that first brush of his lips against hers had left her stunned. And breathless.

She always enjoyed sex well enough, but she generally avoided kissing for she'd never enjoyed it much at all. But those few moments in Harrison's arms had been extraordinary, in a way that went beyond the physical. Never before had a mere kiss felt so powerful, so…invasive. As if he'd found the secret door to her private self and stepped inside.

It had been hours since that kiss, yet the memory of it still lingered on her lips and her body continued to ache for the feel of his own hard form pressed against hers. Would his hands be rough or gentle? Would he enter her hard and fast, or long and slow? The questions persisted, her body aching to know.

Shaking her head, she fought to dislodge the sensuous thoughts from her mind, hating for anyone to have this kind of hold on her. Yet she seemed incapable of shutting him out. With a groan, she shifted yet again, trying to force her thoughts on to the far more pressing matter of Rith and how to get those stones before he did.

A crash sounded outside the window on the street far below. The crumpling of metal and the shattering of glass reverberated into the night. Vehicles colliding? The sound echoed.... No, not echoed. Another crash. And another. And another.

Ilaria's heart began to pound with the certainty something was wrong. Terribly wrong. She struggled against the cuffs that bound her to the bed.

"Human!"

Beneath the crashes another sound, a deep,

rumbling whine pierced the night, followed moments later by an explosion that shook the walls and rattled the windows, vibrating through both the building and the bed.

"Harrison!"

He stormed into the room as she yelled his name, his hair sexily rumpled, his face a bitter mask. The key to her handcuffs was already between his fingers.

"What's happening?" she demanded as he bent over her, unfastening her wrist.

"Armageddon." In the dim light coming through the blinds, she saw a mix of alarm and fury in his eyes. "This is King Rith's doing. Ten bucks says he's found those stones."

Chapter 6

As Harrison freed Ilaria, the handcuffs slipped out of his unsteady hold, hitting the floor behind the bed with a clatter. His heart pounded from being awakened so suddenly, so horrifyingly. And from the fear that this was just the beginning.

Ignoring the fallen cuffs, he straightened and yanked up the shade of the nearest window as the princess rose to stand beside him.

It was like looking at a scene from a disaster movie. Below, streetlights cast their eerie glow on a patchwork of car accidents. Though the sun had yet to rise, the commuters had begun their early morning treks to work. Treks that had ended disastrously. Vehicles were overturned, smoking, piled into one another in every which way. As if no one had tried to stop. As if every one of the drivers had fallen asleep.

Cold chills raced over his skin while his ears buzzed with a harsh white noise. He suspected they had.

A few blocks away, fire glowed orange against the night sky even as another explosion rocked the night in the distance, a fireball erupting in a red glow over D.C. Something had crashed. A helicopter? An airplane?

Good God.

Distant sirens broke through his shock, but close by, nothing stirred. No screams or shouts broke the unnatural quiet. Nothing moved. The only people visible were lying on the street or hanging half out of cars, unconscious. Or dead.

He'd seen this kind of mass enchantment before, six months ago when the Esri, Baleris, found the lost gate into the human world while following the magical scent of the draggon stone. The stone had been doing time as an artifact in the Smithsonian until Baleris stole it.

A sick knot fisted in Harrison's stomach, a

headache began to throb between his eyes as the memory of that day at the Kennedy Center blasted its way through his head. Baleris had sung his tuneless song and everyone—*everyone*—had instantly blacked out, falling unconscious before rising like zombies. Everyone except for his kids and him. And Larsen.

Every instinct he possessed screamed that it had happened again. King Rith or one of his minions had sung a song of enchantment so powerful that drivers had fallen asleep at the wheel and pilots and their craft had fallen out of the sky. Would those who'd survived rise, enchanted? His flesh crawled at the thought of an entire city of controlled humans.

Or would they remain like this…asleep? He didn't know. All he knew was that the stones had been hidden in two different places—the draggon stone and three of the green stones in the water off Ft. McNair. The remaining three green stones in the water off Bolling Air Force Base. The two bases were just across the water from Crystal City. Within two miles of where he was now.

Had King Rith knocked out everyone within a two-mile radius? *Heaven help them.*

"You *idiots.*" Ilaria's quiet exclamation wrenched his attention away from the window. She hit his arm with a small fist, her face a mask of fury. "You foolish, *arrogant* humans—so certain your paltry efforts to hide the stones from Rith would be adequate, while you chained me, *the rightful queen of Esria,* like a beast!"

Teeth clenched tight, she turned back to the window, staring at the destruction. "You will get me to the gate and you'll get me there at once, Harrison, for I've no doubt Rith means to escape back to Esria before anyone can stop him." She whirled back to him. "The moment he reaches the Dark Mountains and the Temple of the Ancients, he'll raise his terrible, unnatural power." Her eyes flashed green fury. "And when those walls come tumbling down, you'll have no one to blame but yourself!"

Harrison didn't interrupt her tirade. He didn't argue at all because, dammit, she was right. He couldn't deny a thing she said.

He turned toward the door. "Come on."

"Where are we going?"

"The gate."

The old feeling of being caught in the middle of a tempest swirled up from deep within the recesses of his bones. The feeling that his world was once more being upended, as it had been when he was thirteen, nearly swamped him—that sense that everything was being ripped out of his control.

It was a feeling he despised.

Crossing the living room, he grabbed his cell phone off the coffee table. As they waited for the elevator, he tried to call Charlie, but the call wouldn't go through. He had a bad feeling the streets were going to be impossible to travel. What they needed was a helicopter.

Then again, if King Rith sang a second time, they didn't want to be in the air. The thought of it turned his blood to ice.

The elevator came quickly and he realized they were almost certainly the only ones in the building awake and walking.

Harrison held the elevator door, letting her

enter first. "King Rith may not have found all seven stones, Ilaria."

"What do you mean?"

"The stones weren't hidden in one place. They were split up. Could he have pulled this much power from just a few of them?"

A thoughtfulness entered her eyes. "I don't know. To my knowledge he's never had his hands on any of them before. My mother guarded the stones carefully."

"Except from you."

"Yes. To her eternal regret."

They took the elevator down to the garage beneath the building. As the doors slid open, the blare of a car horn tore through his eardrums. Harrison held Ilaria back, pushing her behind him. But he saw no movement and heard nothing but the horn.

"Let's go."

Together they made their way across the garage toward the space where he'd parked his car a few hours before. As they rounded the corner, he saw the source of the racket. An old minivan had crashed into one of the concrete uprights, and crashed hard, by the looks of it. The driver, a young woman, lay across the steering wheel, a trickle of blood running down her cheek from her temple. In the backseat, a toddler slept, or lay unconscious, in her car seat.

His stomach clenched, his fatherly instincts leaping. They needed to reach the Dupont Circle fountain as quickly as possible, yet no way could he walk away from a child in need. He started toward the minivan, surprised to find Ilaria right beside him, her face set in worried lines.

"I have some healing skill," she said, as if reading his thoughts…or sharing them.

He glanced at her, seeing a startling compassion in her eyes, and nodded. "We can't help everyone who needs it. There are too many."

"We can help these two." Her quiet words held a thread of steel. Their eyes met. For once they were in complete accord.

"Get the child," he said as they reached the van. Ilaria would never have the strength to lift the woman out.

As she reached for the back door, Harrison wrenched open the front. He pulled the woman off the horn, the night turning blessedly silent, then pressed his fingers to her neck, checking for a pulse. Nice and strong. He unfastened her seat belt while Ilaria climbed in the back. Out of the corner of his eye, he saw her pulling ineffectually at the car-seat straps that pinned a dark-haired little girl.

"The belt release should be between her legs," he told her. "Press the red button and lift the straps up and over her head."

He pulled the woman free from the seat, lifted her out and laid her on the pavement. As Ilaria backed out of the car and turned, the child in her arms, he stilled. For one horrible moment, the child was Stephie, the pale hands holding her, Baleris's.

Stephie's screams tore through his memory, echoing over and over as his stomach clenched with cold fury. For one tense moment he nearly lunged at Ilaria, the need to rip the child out of her pale hands almost more than he could control.

Ilaria froze, the girl cradled tightly against her. Protectively.

"Harrison?" the princess asked softly.

His gaze lifted to hers, to eyes filled with neither malevolent intent nor cruelty, but warm with compassion, and the fury inside him drained away. Something inside him shifted. Ilaria. Not Baleris, not King Rith. Not pale, homogeneous evil. They weren't all alike any more than humans were. He knew that. Kade had shown himself to be good and honorable, even when ordered by his king to kill the Sitheen.

He supposed he hadn't been sure exactly where Ilaria stood on that line between good and evil. Perhaps he still wasn't, but he was a damn sight closer to understanding her. No one who insisted on saving a child could be all bad.

With a last wary look at him, Ilaria laid the child beside her mother, then moved to squat at their heads. As she lifted her hands, she eyed him with question.

"I can help them."

He stared at her, unsettled by his momentary lapse of control. But as he looked into her eyes—into Ilaria's eyes—he trusted her to do what she could. He *trusted* her.

He nodded and she placed a pale hand on each

of the pair's foreheads, the color difference startling.

"How badly are they injured?"

Ilaria's brows drew together. "The child not at all, but the woman hit her head. I feel a trauma." Her gaze widened, a startled, almost wondrous look on her face.

"What's the matter?" he demanded.

"Nothing. They're not Sitheen. Touching them allows me access to their memories, their knowledge. I understand your world, finally. *Incredible.* The things you've accomplished."

"It doesn't hurt them when you do that." It wasn't even a question because he already knew the answer.

She frowned slightly as she watched him. "No." Closing her eyes, her face became a mask of concentration. "*There.* The trauma is gone now."

"You healed her?"

Her lashes swept up. "Yes."

He nodded, a warmth engulfing him. "Good. Thank you."

She studied him with enigmatic eyes, as if uncertain if his attitude toward her had really changed. Slowly, her mouth kicked up in that impish smile, her lips parting as if to speak. But whatever she was going to say was silenced as the mother-daughter pair began to stir.

The woman blinked groggily, struggling to sit up. "What happened?"

"Mommy?"

The woman's hand reached for the child, pulling her against her. Beyond the parking garage the sound of a scream rent the air. Shouting and cries and confused voices soon followed. Everyone was starting to wake. And not as enchanted zombies, thankfully.

"You're safe," Harrison assured the pair. "You had an accident. A lot of people passed out. We're not sure what happened." Which was true enough.

"You look like a princess." The little girl's wide eyes were fixed on Ilaria.

A genuine smile spread across Ilaria's face, sending Harrison's pulse throbbing. "I am a princess, little one."

"A *fairy* princess?"

"Yes, indeed. A real one."

A fairy princess. Good God.

"I'm Princess Ilaria from the land of Esria." She placed her hand on the child's head and smiled. "Be well."

He stared at her, feeling like everything he'd ever understood of good and evil had just been flipped end over end. Humans had once thought them angels, she'd said. And, heaven help him, in that moment he understood why.

Without thinking, he held out his hand for her. "We need to go."

The light still dancing in her eyes, she placed her hand in his and allowed him to help her up.

As his fingers closed around hers, their gazes locked, awareness arcing between them. And a deep, surprising warmth. Once again, he felt himself falling into that green gaze, right through the door to her soul. A soul untainted by darkness or evil. He felt encompassed in a brightness that drew him on the most fundamental level.

Her lips curled upward ever so slightly and it was all he could do not to pull her back into his arms. But this was neither the time nor the place. With a shake of his head, he broke eye contact and led her through the garage to where he'd parked his car. But a glance at the entrance disabused him of any thought of driving out of there. From where he stood he could see three vehicles, including a delivery truck, blocking the entrance in one impressive tangle.

"What do we do now?" Ilaria asked, her gaze following his.

"I'm not sure. We could try the metro, but God only knows what kind of mess this caused underground. We'll have to walk until things open up."

"How far is the gate?"

"Miles from here. Hopefully we'll be able to find a cab or a ride, at some point."

Together they made their way out of the garage, past the wreckage, and into a scene of confusion and terror. Some of the people who'd been lying in the street or in the cars now stumbled, injured and confused. Others screamed or shouted, or ran, seeking help. Others remained where they'd landed. Not everyone had regained consciousness. Some never would.

In the distance the flicker of flames licked at the night sky from a source he couldn't see.

"Ilaria..." He glanced at her to find her staring at that distant fire, too. She didn't seem to have heard him. "Ilaria, I need to ask you something."

She shook her head, as if shaking herself loose from some dark thought, then glanced at him.

The words caught in his throat. "My daughter...Stephie..."

"You're mated...married?"

"No. Not for years. But I have two kids, a nine-year-old-son, Sam, and a seven-year-old daughter." Why was he telling her this? If the Esri figured out, rightly, that his kids were Sitheen, they could all the more easily hunt them down. But he knew why he was telling her. Watching her with that other child, something had changed. "Baleris touched my daughter...all he did was touch her head. I was there. I saw it. But she started screaming and when she stopped..." His jaw clenched tight. "She's not there anymore. She's alive, but...not there."

"You're wondering if I could help her."

"Yes." Good God, could he really let another Esri touch her? Would he honestly ask Gwen to bring her down here, to risk her life? Hell, what life? "Yes. Could you heal her? If I brought her to you?"

"I don't know. I have some healing skill with simple things. It depends on what Baleris did to her. But I'll try, Harrison. Of course, I'll try."

He nodded once, a perfunctory move as his fatherly instincts rose up, shouting at him that he was out of his mind. But what if Ilaria could help? What if she could give him his daughter back?

He sure as hell couldn't ask Gwen to bring her down here now, not the way things were. Not with King Rith on his rampage. But they'd get that bastard. He had to believe they'd stop him as they had the other Esri before him. And once they did, before Ilaria left, sealing the gates behind her, he'd bring Stephie to her.

A truck rumbled by, inching through the wreckage. Harrison took Ilaria's hand, pulling her with him down the sidewalk. In the distance, the sirens grew louder, making him think the entire area hadn't been affected. Those outside the war zone were coming to the rescue. But with the mess the roads were in, they wouldn't be making progress very fast.

As a car approached, Harrison held out his hand to flag the guy down, but the driver ignored him. For once, he wished he carried a gun. He had a bad feeling it might take that to get a car. Especially paired, as he was, with a woman who in no way looked normal.

"We might have better luck if you use a little glamour," he told her.

"Who would they stop for? A child? An injured woman?"

He hadn't even thought about that. "A cop."

As the next car approached, Ilaria held out her hand and the car came to an immediate halt. A middle-aged man with a significant bald spot rolled down the window. "What the hell happened, Officer?"

Ilaria went to him, touching the hand that rested on the open window. "You'll leave your car and go to help the people who are injured."

The man's eyes glazed over. He opened the car door and the car started to roll.

Harrison grabbed Ilaria's shoulder. "Put the car in Park, first!"

Ilaria repeated the words and the man slammed

his foot on the brake and did as she commanded, then climbed out and walked away, leaving the car idling.

Ilaria ran for the passenger door as Harrison climbed in the driver's side. "Good work." He pushed the seat back to accommodate his longer legs. "I never thought I'd see the day when I was glad to have an Esri for a partner."

She glanced at him with enigmatic eyes. "Just get us to that gate, human."

Harrison smiled grimly.

For the next hour, they worked their way through Crystal City, driving when there was an open space in the road, walking when they had to, then enchanting another driver into helping them again. He kept looking for a motorcyclist, but so far, they'd been in short supply. Time after time, they passed a person in need of help, but he forced himself to focus on the thing that mattered most, on the one thing they could do that would make the biggest difference. They had to reach Dupont Circle before King Rith opened that gate.

They were on the 14th Street bridge when his phone finally rang. He grabbed it.

"Hello?"

Charlie's voice came through strong and clear. "King Rith attacked Fort McNair. He found the three green stones we'd hidden there and apparently knocked out everyone nearby."

"I'm fully aware of the last part," Harrison muttered.

"You got hit, too?"

"Looks like the end of days in Crystal City."

"Kade talked to Autumn. The Adams Morgan area is fine. Best we can figure, he took out everyone within about a two-mile radius of Fort McNair."

"You think he did all this with just three stones?"

"We're ninety-percent sure he didn't get the others. The only way to be one hundred percent certain is to pull them out and look at them, but that will just give him a lock on them. We've talked to the Sitheen recruit posted at Bolling. There's been no sign of Esri over there."

"Paige was the one guarding the ones at Fort McNair, wasn't she?"

Charlie didn't answer immediately and when

he did, his voice was grave. "She phoned Jack the moment they spotted the Esri. The delivery van the bastards hid inside didn't stop at the gate, so the MPs shot out the tires. That's when all hell broke loose. A dozen Esri leaped from the van carrying swords. The flamethrowers were useless against them, thanks to King Rith's ability to douse fire. The only reason you guys were able to use them the other night, apparently, was that the bastard ran and didn't bother to put them out. Tonight he did. The Esri cut down every man in their path. And every woman."

Harrison felt a kick in the gut. "Paige is dead."

"Yes."

Dammit. He'd only known her a couple weeks, but she'd been strong and decent. "Any other Sitheen?"

"No, and no Esri deaths. Once King Rith got the stones and sang, not even the holly worked. Every human on that base lost consciousness. There was no one to stop them on the way out."

Harrison gripped the steering wheel hard. "He's on his way to Bolling."

"We think so, too, but we can't get there to defend it. Not with the death marks. If he hasn't figured out where the other stones are, we'll lead him right to them. Getting rid of these death marks has become priority number one. We need you to bring Ilaria to McNair."

"You think raising the draggon stone is worth the risk?"

"If we don't, we're not only sitting ducks, but useless. Once Ilaria's done with the stone, we'll hide it beneath one of the boats and move it. It was in the water at McNair, not far from the other three, yet we've reason to believe King Rith didn't find it. He apparently can't sense that one like he can the others."

A mere stone scenter wouldn't have been able to find any of the stones through the lead-lined boxes hiding beneath the surface of the Anacostia River. Fortunately, Rith's Caller abilities apparently only worked on the lesser stones, not the draggon. Unfortunately, once they pulled the draggon out of its hiding place, Rith, like any stone scenter, would be able to follow the magical scent.

"I'll get Ilaria over there as fast as I can."

"Call me when you're close."

"Will do." Harrison snapped his phone closed and looked at Ilaria. "How much of that could you hear?"

"All of it."

"That's what I was afraid of." Traffic was moving, if not quickly, so they stayed in the car, easing around a delivery van smashed up against the rail. "How well do you know King Rith?"

"Not well. After my first centuries, I spent little time in the Fair Court. Fifteen hundred years ago, I returned for a short while, to discover my mother had taken a new consort. Rith. I have a rare ability to sense power in others and I knew at once he had the markings of a dark Caller. I told the queen, but she was enamored of him and ordered me out of the Fair Court. She had no use for me or my complaints, as she called them. I stole the seven stones and ran."

"It sounds like you didn't have a lot of respect for your mother."

"I didn't." She raked a frustrated hand through her hair. "Don't get me wrong. I loved her. But she never saw the crown as a responsibility, only a privilege, and was concerned exclusively with her own needs and wishes. It was my mother who first enslaved the humans, then turned on the Marceils when the humans were lost to us after I sealed the gates. She wasn't intentionally cruel, she simply never considered anyone but herself."

"You disapproved of the enslavement?"

She exhaled a sharp breath. "The Esri don't need slaves. Ours is a simple world. A small bit of work is all it takes to live in comfort, but my mother wanted all things given to her. And her couriers and ladies learned to desire the same."

Harrison enjoyed the sound of her words, hearing the frustration and regret as she painted the picture of a strong-willed, honorable heroine in a larger-than-life family drama. A fairy princess thwarting her queen mother and the evil consort who meant to take advantage. But what was the truth? Was she intentionally painting herself in a heroic light? Or merely recounting the past as she remembered it? Or was she out-and-out lying to him for another purpose altogether?

How could he ever know?

They finally managed to get through the mess

on the bridge, only to come to a standstill as he tried to turn onto Maine Avenue. Ahead, an accident had the road entirely blocked. They'd reached the end of the line.

Harrison stopped the car and turned off the ignition, leaving the keys inside. "Time to walk again."

They climbed out and into a scene he knew would be imprinted on his mind for years to come. A bus appeared to have been split in half by a pair of trash trucks that had come at it from either side. Bodies and refuse were strewn everywhere.

Ilaria's palm went to her forehead as he steered her through the wreckage. God, he was going to be sick. Every inch of his skin turned hot, then cold, then clammy, his stomach twisting, his muscles aching. He didn't think he'd ever get used to seeing death like this. He'd never been a soldier, never gravitated toward battlefields, either foreign or urban. His world, until six months ago, had been filled with computers and clients and staff meetings. Not until Baleris found his way through the gate had death become a part of his life.

They'd only gone a short distance when Ilaria grabbed him, her slender fingers curling around his wrist with surprising strength.

"Harrison. Up ahead. *Esri.*"

Chapter 7

Harrison knew the moment the two Esri spotted the princess. Their steps faltered, their eyes widened and their jaws dropped in tandem. There was no mistaking them as anything but Esri, with their pale skin and hair, and their matching uniforms of black pants and silver tunics. But side by side the pair looked nothing alike. One was the color of snow and sported a mass of long yellowish curls, like something out of a British courtroom drama. The other's skin was darker, closer to the ivory color of Ilaria's, his long, straight hair the same shade, his face thin and sharp.

As one, they started toward Ilaria. Harrison's hand dove into his pocket, his fingers closing around one of the Bic lighters he never went without anymore. He wished to hell he had a flamethrower instead.

"I know them," Ilaria said softly at his side.

Hell. But after two thousand years, she probably knew most Esri.

"The one on the right," she said, indicating the darker-skinned one, "is Luciar. He was a loyal member of my mother's guard for more than a millennia. The other, Sanderis, was a member of her guard in later years."

"Friends of yours, by any chance?"

"No. But they were part of my mother's guard. Just because they serve King Rith now doesn't mean they won't shift their loyalty to me now that I'm free."

"Neither does it mean they will."

"True. But they've seen me, Harrison. If I run now, they'll give chase, either to capture me or rescue me. We have to play this out." She reached for him, squeezing his wrist. "Pretend to be enchanted. And whatever you do, don't kill them. If Rith and the rest of his guard are nearby, the death mark will bring them running. You could endanger us both."

He couldn't deny the soundness of her logic, but the thought of pretending to be enchanted… *mindless*…and letting her lead him to the guards appalled him. Yet his only other choice was to let them know he was Sitheen, which would lead to a fight to the death.

Because no way was he letting her get anywhere near them without him.

He supposed he was going to have to find it within himself to put on an act worthy of an Oscar.

"Stay behind me, Ilaria."

"No. You're enchanted, remember? You can't speak again unless I tell you to."

He growled low, earning another warning squeeze of his wrist, but her fingers caressed after they squeezed, sending tendrils of warmth sliding over his skin.

With a struggle, he cleared his face of all emotion. Through what he hoped were dull eyes, he watched the pair approach.

Neither Esri gave away a single thought through his expression. They'd make damn good poker players, which was the last thing Harrison needed right now. The closer they came, the faster his pulse raced, and the more he had to struggle to unclench his jaw and to keep the growing hatred out of his eyes.

The hand in his pocket stroked the lighter.

Though each guard glanced at him, neither paid him much attention. His attempt to appear witless seemed to be working. While that relieved him immeasurably on one level, it annoyed the heck out of him on another. *Witless, my ass.*

"Princess Ilaria," Luciar exclaimed softly, his eyes lighting with what appeared to be genuine pleasure. He bowed low, as did his companion. "How did you ever get free?" he asked, rising again to a height comparable with Harrison's own.

Out of the corner of his eye, Harrison watched Ilaria's expression turn regal and cool. Wary.

Good girl.

"The gates opened," she said simply, allowing the pair to think what they would.

"Sweet Esria, I'm glad you're free," Sanderis exclaimed. "King Rith…" He shook his head, as if that said it all.

Along his wrist, Harrison felt Ilaria's fingers spasm. With relief that these men were loyal to her? Dismay that she'd seen through them? Or regret that she was about to turn them on the human at her side? No. Not the last. She wouldn't betray him.

Still, he wished to hell he knew what was going on in her head because this homecoming wasn't going down as he'd expected. The guards weren't prostrating themselves for their rightful queen, or greeting her with warm hugs. Nor were they grabbing her in order to drag her to King Rith.

By the tension in Ilaria's hand and the coolness of her tone, he suspected she couldn't tell what their game was any better than he could.

"We cannot allow King Rith to find you, Princess," Luciar said. "He'll never allow you to return to Esria."

"He'll not risk you stealing his throne," the other agreed.

Ilaria's chin lifted ever so slightly. "Rith is a Caller." The words sounded as both accusation and command.

Sanderis's eyes narrowed, his brows lowering as if dismayed. "Why would you say that?"

"How can you doubt it?" Ilaria snapped. "All you have to do is look around you. This is Rith's doing."

Luciar had turned away before Harrison caught his reaction, but now he turned back with an expression of remorse. "I've suspected he was a Caller for a while, but never had proof."

Ilaria eyed him sharply. "How many of the stones are in his possession?"

"Three."

"Can you imagine what will happen if he gets his hands on all seven?"

Excitement flared in Luciar's eyes for a split second before he dampened it, but not before Harrison saw. The thought of even greater destruction excited the bastard. Which meant he was no friend to Ilaria.

"We'll have to confront him, Princess," Luciar said with a gravity that proved him a fine actor. "We've a safe place to hide you where he won't find you. Leave your human here. You won't need him."

Don't trust him, Ilaria. If only it was his hand on *her* wrist, he might be able to warn her.

Sanderis's gaze slid to Luciar, then down to his own feet. Sanderis knew what Luciar was up to. Harrison's muscles tensed. Ilaria's fingers clenched around his wrist, but whether in response to his tension or to Luciar's words, he couldn't tell.

"I want my draggon stone, Luciar." A queen commanding her subjects.

Luciar dipped his head in acknowledgement. "You'll have them all, Princess. My queen," he amended, his voice so rich with sincerity that Harrison's conviction that he'd seen subterfuge wavered. "Now, let's get you hidden before King Rith comes upon us."

But as Luciar spoke, he slipped Sanderis a look that had every muscle in Harrison's body going rigid. He'd spent too many years across the negotiating table to not recognize silent communication passing between the pair. A communication that boded ill.

She wasn't going anywhere with these two. He'd take a death mark before he'd allow it.

But as Luciar reached for her, Ilaria stepped back, pulling Harrison with her. "I'm safer on my own, Luciar, and we both know it."

Luciar's eyes turned hard. "I must insist you come with us, Princess. We are most concerned with your safety."

"Are you?" Ilaria asked coolly. "Who were the traitors who turned on my mother, your queen, Luciar?"

The Esri's mouth flattened. Again, he flicked his gaze toward Sanderis. Harrison tensed, unsurprised when a second later they lunged.

Sanderis flattened his palm against Harrison's shoulder as if to push him away, but Harrison grabbed the Esri's arm, using the man's momentum to flip him. As Sanderis sprawled on the sidewalk, Harrison turned to Luciar. But his plan to tackle him was dashed when the Esri pulled a wicked-looking knife.

Ilaria glided between them, her back to Harrison as if to protect him. But even as she moved, Sanderis leaped to his feet, a knife in his hands, too. The Esri were definitely learning how to dispatch Sitheen. Enchantment might not work, but good old-fashioned violence would, every time.

"Harrison, run! *Please.*"

Instead, he feinted toward Sanderis, drawing a stab which he easily avoided. The moment the Esri's arm was extended, Harrison latched onto his wrist, immobilizing his knife hand as he pulled his Bic lighter, flicked it, and shoved the fire into Sanderis's flesh. Instantly, the Esri went up in flame.

He swung back toward Luciar only to find him hauling Ilaria against him, using her as a shield. A nasty smile pulled at the Esri guard's mouth. "Set me on fire and you'll burn us both. But I don't think you want to do that, *Sitheen.*"

Ilaria clung to the arm locked across her shoulders. *Clung.* It was a moment before the look on her face registered. She was staring at the screaming Sanderis, terrified. *Terrified.* As if she fully expected Harrison to turn on her, too.

The realization was a fist to the gut. Did she really think him that much of a monster?

Watching him with cunning eyes, Luciar opened his mouth and started to sing. Not the death chant, but neither was it music. No one would ever mistake it for music. It was a cry that, had Harrison heard it in the wild he might have thought it some kind of animal mating call. It sounded eerily like the song Baleris had sung at the Kennedy Center that day.

He tensed, waiting for the humans to collapse once more. Instead, they started walking toward him. More than two dozen men, women and children moved to encircle them. Somehow Luciar had skipped the unconscious step and gone straight to zombies.

Not a mating call, a call to action. To destruction. He had no doubt that the moment they reached him, they'd attack him like a pack of wild dogs, pummeling, kicking, clawing until all that remained of him was a bloody stain on the pavement.

If he didn't get out of here *now,* he never would. But he wasn't leaving Ilaria behind.

He launched himself at Luciar, tackling both him and Ilaria to the ground as he sought to free her from the bastard. The knife clattered away, but Luciar's grip only slid upward, going tight around her neck.

For one terrible moment, Harrison thought the guard was going to choke her until logic returned. She was immortal. Luciar couldn't hurt her, couldn't strangle her, no matter what it looked like to Harrison's human eyes.

Grabbing Luciar's face with one hand, Harrison slammed the Esri's skull back into the pavement over and over again while he clawed at his arm, trying to free Ilaria.

He looked at her, dismayed to see her eyes still glazed with fear.

"Ilaria, I'm trying to help you. Fight him!"

Her gaze focused on him slowly, clinging to him. Finally she moved, her hands grabbing the arm at her neck and between the two of them they set her free. As she scrambled to her feet, Harrison shoved the lighter into Luciar's flesh and leaped back as the second Esri turned to flame. Around him, the zombies stopped abruptly, collapsing to the ground, some only a few yards away.

Close. Too close.

He stared at Luciar, so tempted to sing the death chant. While he might be willing to risk his own life, acquiring a death mark would endanger Ilaria. Not a risk he was willing to take.

He grabbed her hand, hating the look of stark terror still wild in her eyes. A terror that calmed ever so slightly when she looked at him. It wasn't him she was afraid of, he realized with a slam of relief. He was almost certain it was the fire.

"Ilaria, we have to go." But she didn't move. He could see the pulse jackhammering at her throat. *"Ilaria."* Gripping her shoulder, he gave her a small shake.

Awareness flared in her eyes. "Yes. Let's go."

The moment the humans came to, they'd be grabbing buckets and hoses and saving those two *poor burning souls*—the monsters who sought to help King Rith enslave the entire human race.

He tugged on her hand and together they set off at a fast walk. When Ilaria began to run beside him, despite her long skirt, he nodded with satisfaction and began to jog. Needing to get them out of the line of sight of the two Esri before they pulled free of the fire, Harrison led her around the corner of one of the restaurants until they were running alongside the waterfront lined with docks.

Watching Luciar grab her had done something to him. The rage he'd felt against the Esri race had coalesced into a single, sharp fury and a primitive need to protect. Not his world, not his mission. *Ilaria.*

His gaze slid to her, unable to stay away. "Mind telling me what happened back there? Was it the fire?"

She glanced at him, echoes of that wild fear still clouding her eyes. "Yes."

"Have you always been afraid of it?"

"Not always, no."

"Want to elaborate?"

"No."

They kept running along the waterfront, then onto a residential street lined with brick apartment buildings and well-maintained homes.

"We have no fire in Esria," Ilaria said, when they were well out of sight of the Esri. "As I'm sure you can imagine, since it's the only thing that can kill us. I was sixteen the first time I visited the human realm. I thought it the most beautiful thing I'd ever seen."

"You touched it."

"I did. And immediately erupted into flame. The humans poured water on me until the fire went out, but it took time. The pain was significant. Being immobilized by it was terrifying."

"Didn't they get suspicious when you weren't hurt?"

"They knew who I was. This particular village worshipped the Esri and treated us as gods."

"I'm surprised you were able to spend any time in this world after that. There must have been fires everywhere."

"There were. That incident gave me a healthy respect for it, I assure you. A fear that sometimes visited my dreams, but wasn't debilitating."

Unlike now. "What happened?"

She met his gaze, a deep trauma alive in her eyes. "The Forest of Nightmares."

He remembered Charlie saying the forest served up your worst nightmares. Good God. It had showed her fire. Perhaps herself burning. For how long? How many times?

Her pale lashes swept down. When they lifted again, the trauma was well contained behind layers of strength and granite determination. She raised her chin, in full control once more. The princess was back. No, not the princess. The queen. And this queen, he had no doubt, would face whatever she must to reclaim her throne.

Ilaria freed her hand from Harrison's and grabbed her skirts, running beside him. Not in centuries and centuries had she seen real fire, and the sight of it, the feel of it, was an assault to her mind and senses that would remain with her for a long, long time. The heat of it still licked at her skin, the sight a white haze of fear that slowly dissipated as her insides shivered like water in a breeze.

But the cold that slowed the blood's flow through her veins was not a result of the fire, but of betrayal. For millennia, Luciar and Sanderis had been loyal to her mother. Loyal to their queen. They should be loyal to her, too, yet they'd been prepared to drag her to King Rith, knowing he'd never allow her to reclaim the throne of Esria.

Neither seemed concerned that Rith was a Caller.

What had he done to them? To all her people. Won their hearts, or their fear? And did it matter, so long as they were loyal to him and not to her?

For years, she'd worried that she might never leave the forest. With her rescue she'd allowed herself to imagine the celebration she'd return to. As the rightful queen.

Now she was beginning to wonder if she'd receive any kind of welcome at all. What lies had Rith told to justify her incarceration? Somehow, she'd never truly allowed herself to believe her people could be turned against her. Now, she was afraid she'd been naive and was doomed to return to Esria a pariah.

The thought fell like a heavy stone upon her heart, yet did nothing to dim her determination. Even if she never reclaimed her throne, even if she found herself again incarcerated within the Forest of Nightmares, she must keep Rith from claiming the seven stones. That was the one thing she could do for her world, for her people. The thing she *must* do in order to keep both worlds safe from the evil Rith intended to inflict upon them all.

"We've lost them," Harrison said at last, slowing to a walk. He took her hand again and led her around the corner of one of the redbrick buildings, then turned her to face him, his hands firm on her shoulders.

His breath was labored, but not unduly so, his expression concerned. "Are you okay?" Those tiny frown lines appeared again between his eyebrows, but this time she welcomed them, knowing they signified his worry for her.

Her heart lightened. How strange that the one who was proving most loyal to her was the very one who, just hours ago, she'd had the most concern about.

She smiled. "I'm okay." Truly, she was more than okay. His loyalty and protectiveness filled her with a sweetness unlike anything she'd ever felt. Perspiration beaded on his brow despite the cold, his cheeks flushed with pink. How was it possible that in such a short time, his face could become so dear?

His hand cupped her cheek, his eyes studying her as if he sought the truth. His touch set up an intense fluttering inside her chest, a tingling warmth. The man was starting to scare her. He was just a human, just a mortal, but he'd touched something within her that no one else ever had. In those brief moments when they'd kissed back in his apartment, she'd felt as if he'd reached inside her mind. As if he'd seen her. And for a brief moment she'd felt as if she wasn't alone in this shell of a body. As if she'd connected to another for the very first time.

As he stared into her eyes now, she felt it again, that disturbing connection. A connection with a man whose entire life would span only a single heartbeat of the world. What a terrible waste for such a man to be mortal. What a cruel trick for fate to put him in her path for only a few short days or weeks. To let her glimpse what she'd been missing, then snatch it away again.

"Had you expected them to be loyal to you?" he asked softly.

Her lips compressed, but she didn't look away. She couldn't have torn her gaze from his in that moment if she'd wanted to. "He's been their king for three-hundred years. Three centuries is a long time, even to us."

"That doesn't answer my question," he said quietly, his words rich with understanding.

She sighed. "I'd hoped."

His hand lifted to brush her hair back from her face in a move so gentle, so caring, she felt tears prick her eyes. "I'm sorry, Ilaria. I know it has to be a blow."

"It's...disappointing." Temper flared inside her. "No, it's infuriating."

He nodded slowly. "I agree." He released her and together they began to walk again.

"After seeing what Rith has done with only three of those stones, they know he's a Caller, yet they support him anyway." She sliced her hand through the air in disgust. "What do they think is going to happen when he comes into his power? Do they think he's going to make them generals? He won't need generals! He'll have complete control of everyone. *Everyone.*"

"Maybe they're just too scared of him not to support him."

"I might believe it of Sanderis, but not Luciar. Luciar was delighted by the prospect of delivering me to Rith, I saw it in his eyes."

"I'm afraid I have to agree with you."

They continued in comfortable silence, the accord between them deepening. Such a short time ago, her plan had been to seduce him and try to manipulate him into getting her the stones. But with Rith's attack, everything had changed.

On every street they found another wrecked vehicle or more evidence of Rith's destruction. There was no need for the humans and Esri to be enemies, but how could the humans not fear and hate their immortal brethren when treated with such callous cruelty? Such disrespect for life?

"How much farther?" she asked after a while.

"A few more blocks. We're almost there." He pulled out his phone and called Charlie. "We'll be there in ten."

"We're waiting," his brother said.

Harrison disconnected the call and glanced at her.

She met his gaze with a fierce determination. "Killing one another isn't our way, Harrison. But if you ever get the chance to kill Rith, you must take it. He's the only known Caller in existence and stopping him is far more important than sealing the gates."

His brows drew down. "What are you saying?"

"Rith will start looking for me the moment Luciar tells him I'm here. If the situation ever arises that Rith grabs me, as Luciar did, don't risk trying to save me. Don't risk losing your chance to stop him."

"You want me to just set you both on fire and sing the death chant?" He said the words simply, without emotion, as if clarifying a minor point. But a muscle leaped in his jaw.

"You must stop him, Harrison. Or both worlds are lost."

For a couple minutes he said nothing, his mouth hard. Finally he spoke. "I get why he's a danger to us, but I don't understand why he's a threat to you."

Her hands clutched at the soft, slick fabric of her skirt. "The draggon stone has existed for as long as the Esri can remember, but the six green stones were created in the Temple of the Ancients only eight thousand years ago. Near history to us. They were created by the last king of Esria, Orisis. My grandfather."

Harrison frowned, but he listened, and she continued. "He was a Caller. One capable of calling dark magic from the draggon stone. Callers have existed in the past, though the talent is rare. Orisis found a way to use the combined power of the temple and the draggon stone to create the six green stones. He claimed they would increase the abundance of the land, and they do. But they do more than that.

"Little by little, he learned to coax the dark magic from them until one day it broke free. The result was terrible. He was able to enslave our entire race, body and will, as the Esri now enslave the Marceils. The Esri knew what he was forcing them to do, yet were helpless to fight it. They became puppets in the hands of an evil master. And Orisis was truly evil.

"For several years, the Esri suffered greatly. But over his long life Orisis had sired two children, a son who would become king after him, and a daughter who would later become my mother. In all of Esria, only Orisis's son was free of his control since he, too, was a Caller. But unlike his father, he had no evil in his heart. When the opportunity finally arose, he killed him."

"He killed his own father," Harrison murmured beside her. "And acquired a death mark."

"Yes."

"You can remove death marks with the help of the stones. He couldn't?"

"Not even a king can remove his own death mark. He kept everyone at bay, terrified they'd try to end him. The only one he let come near was his sister, my mother, which proved his last mistake. My mother never cared for anyone but herself."

"But she didn't acquire a death mark because there's no penalty for killing one already marked for death."

"Correct. My mother became queen and decreed that Callers were not to be suffered. Anyone killing one would be cleared of their death mark. Only a couple of Callers have been discovered since and they've both been ended. Until Rith. Unfortunately, the ability to sense that kind of power in others is an extremely rare gift, which, in recent centuries, has become far more rare. Shortly before I sealed the gates, before I met Rith and realized what he was, several Esri who were known to be able to sense power in others got caught and were killed during the Sitheen wars in the human world."

"Killed by Sitheen. By humans."

"Yes. I've always suspected Rith arranged their deaths."

"So they couldn't betray the truth of what he was."

Ilaria nodded. "But Rith didn't know about me or about my gift. I'd never made it known that I was able to sense power, for my gift was never a strong one. After I stole the stones from my mother, I brought them here and sealed the gates, where Rith would never find them. I tried to convince my mother that he was a Caller, but she refused to listen and it didn't seem to matter any longer. And for a long time, it didn't."

"Until he had her killed and then imprisoned

you in the Forest of Nightmares. Why did he wait so long? Nearly twelve hundred years."

"I don't know." But she did. At least she was all too afraid she did. Without the draggon stone, her mother's power had weakened. Slowly. Ever so slowly, until finally Rith was able to move against her. But if she admitted the truth to Harrison, he'd realize she wouldn't leave the draggon stone behind this time. Once she came into her power, she'd not release the stone again.

She glanced at him as they walked. "If he gets his hands on all seven stones, or even just the six dark ones, he'll be unstoppable. That's why he must be destroyed, no matter the cost."

His gaze met hers, his eyes piercing. "I'm not going to set you on fire, Ilaria. It's not going to come to that."

"You can't know…."

"Yes. I can. I'm not going to let it come to that." His words rang of truth and a conviction she'd rarely heard in another. "We didn't bring you here to let you die."

"Be ever mindful of the greater good, Harrison. Never forget it."

"I don't intend to." His eyes crinkled, a smile lighting their depths even though his mouth didn't move.

She returned the small smile, warmed all over again. He was a rare man, this one. But as she'd warned him not to lose sight of the greater good, neither could she. And the knowledge twisted sickly inside her. Because everything she'd said was true. Rith must be stopped at any cost. And if the only way for her to get the remaining stones and flee to Esria before Rith caught her meant the death of any or all of the Sitheen, then they would die. She'd have no choice.

She could only hope it didn't come to that, because the more time she spent with this human, the less she wanted to see him hurt. Within his chest beat the heart of a man of loyalty and honor. A man who, despite a sharp hatred of her kind, treated her with more respect than her own people did.

Of all those in either world she could fight this battle beside, she would choose him.

Until the time came that she must betray him.

Chapter 8

It was midmorning by the time Harrison and Ilaria finally reached Ft. McNair, the day cold and gray. At the gate, they found a car waiting for them and Harrison ushered her into the backseat, then followed her in.

Ilaria gazed out the window, curious about this place they called a fort. She'd anticipated a grand castle or fortress, but the reality was far less imposing. Fenced, yes, but otherwise merely a small collection of low buildings surrounding a wide, grassy area. The term *drill field* came to mind, though what a drill field was, she didn't know.

Dotting the field and the perimeter road were puddles of dark fluid. Dozens of them.

Even as she frowned, understanding swept over her with an ice-cold chill.

Blood, each puddle evidence of another human death. So many puddles. So many dead.

It was a wonder the humans didn't kill every Esri they met on sight. But the human race, at least those she'd known, had always been a mix of the wise and the fearful. It was her good fortune, and possibly that of their entire race, that the Sitheen appeared to be made up of the former. Wise, strong men and women who fought to save their world.

Wise enough to understand that the only way to stop Rith was to take the stones back to Esria and destroy them? She was afraid they wouldn't accept that answer. She feared they'd see it as betrayal. Even Harrison. Especially Harrison.

Maybe it wouldn't come to that. If she'd sensed anything from this group, it was that they didn't give up. She wasn't sure what chance they stood against Rith now that he had the power of three of the stones, but they'd succeeded against other Esri, other foes.

Maybe, just maybe, they'd defeat Rith, too.

Then destroying the stones would no longer be of critical importance. As queen, she might be able to build some trust between the races, perhaps enough trust to reclaim the stones without a fight.

All she could do now was try to earn the Sitheen's trust while she aided them in beating Rith in any way she could.

And pray it was enough.

The car came to a stop. "They're over by the water," the driver told them.

As she climbed from the car, she was hit by a startling thrill of power that danced over her skin, calling to her. *The draggon stone*. She'd always been drawn to its power through her royal blood. But never before had she felt it call to her in return, as if seeking its true queen. Her pulse leaped with anticipation at the prospect of holding it at last.

What gifts might it bestow upon her? She'd heard it rumored that many of her mother's unique talents—the ability to communicate telepathically, the ability to inflict pain with a wave of her hand—came to her through the draggon stone. As a child, Ilaria had wondered why the draggon stone didn't give *her* gifts as it had her mother. It wasn't until later that she'd learned that such gifts, if they came, were bestowed when a new king or queen came into his or her power. A *rightful* king or queen.

Would that happen today? Here?

"What's the matter?" Harrison asked as they met at the rear of the car, his gaze sharp on her face. "Something happened."

She thought about prevaricating, then decided there was no need. "I can feel the draggon stone."

His expression turned probing and intent. "Can you sense all the stones or just the draggon?"

Was that wariness she saw in his eyes? Her mouth compressed. "Only the draggon, the stone of royalty. The other six, the stones of Orisis, don't call to me. They never have."

He nodded, then turned to where Charlie and three others waited, but he made no move toward them. She was all too afraid she knew why.

"You do realize I have to touch them to remove their death marks," she said quietly.

His gaze swung back to her, more troubled than wary, she realized. "I know. I trust you."

An unspoken *but* lingered in the air between them—the knowledge that if that trust was misplaced, she could destroy his brother. And his friends.

"Your trust is not misplaced, Harrison." It was on the tip of her tongue to add, *I won't hurt them.* But she couldn't. Though she meant them no harm here and now, that was a promise she could make neither of them. "Trust me to remove their death marks as I said I would."

He watched her a moment more, his eyes probing as if they sought the secrets of her soul. Finally, he took a deep breath and let it out slowly, then nodded.

She tried to smile, but the smile wouldn't come. "Thank you." She prayed his trust was warranted. But what the next hours would bring, none of them could know.

Harrison took her hand and led her across a wide strip of brown grass toward the four people standing beneath one of the winter-bare trees that lined the water's edge. She recognized Charlie and the tall, dark-haired Esri, Kaderil. She assumed the other two were Jack and Larsen.

"Kaderil is truly loyal to the human cause?" she asked quietly.

"All indications are he's loyal. Do you remember the tall redhead who greeted Tarrys when we dropped her off? The woman's name is Autumn. Kade's asked her to marry him."

Ilaria's jaw dropped. "How…?"

"Rith sent Kade to infiltrate the Sitheen, steal the draggon stone, which was the only one we had at the time, then kill us. Lucky for us, Autumn was the first one he met. She may be human, but there's no denying the woman enchanted him."

"He loves her."

"Apparently."

Kaderil the Dark had possessed a reputation for violence that had terrified most within Esria. That he'd joined forces with humans, and fallen in love, was nothing short of extraordinary. Unless…he'd merely infiltrated their ranks. Was he still working for Rith?

All four carried what appeared to be weapons of some kind.

"What do their weapons do?" she asked Harrison.

"They're flamethrowers. Each shoots a stream of fire."

Just the thought of such a weapon sent a chill shooting down her spine.

Harrison's hand tightened around hers. "Easy. They won't use them unless Rith and his goons show up again."

As they approached the group, Charlie's gaze went from Harrison to her and back again, a smile hovering at the corners of his mouth.

"Princess," Charlie said, meeting her gaze with a nod.

The male she didn't know inclined his head. "I'm Jack Hallihan, Princess."

The woman did the same. "Larsen Hallihan."

Charlie's gaze dropped to Harrison and Ilaria's joined hands. "What'd she do, bro, enchant you? Not a handcuff in sight."

"Armageddon woke me from a sound sleep. Forgive me if I got a little distracted. Besides, as Ilaria has reminded me, she has to touch you to remove your death marks. We either trust her or we don't. There's no halfway."

Charlie lifted a brow. "And you've decided you trust her?"

"I have."

To her surprise, Charlie's expression grew serious, a look of satisfaction easing the lines of his face. "Good. So let's do this."

"I agree." Kaderil stepped forward, giving her a formal bow. "Princess Ilaria. I'm glad to see you free, at last."

"Thank you, Kaderil. I'm glad to be free." She'd seen him a time or two, many centuries ago. With his human coloring and great height, he was not a man one forgot.

"You suffered no ill effects from the forest?" His concern seemed genuine and she wondered if he was proving a point to the others, or trying to get a read on her himself. She had no doubt those who crossed him had reason to fear him, but she was beginning to think there was more depth to this man than most Esri, including herself, had realized.

"There was a clearing in the middle of the forest where the old Marceillian temple stood," she told him. "We lived there, free from the forest's attacks." She tried to hide a shudder. "If not for the clearing, I'd have gone mad long, long ago, I assure you."

"I understand that completely," Charlie muttered.

Ilaria eyed the dark Esri. "You betray your king by aiding the Sitheen, Kaderil."

The big man nodded, calm certainty in his eyes. "King Rith would destroy this world. I fight with the humans to stop him."

"And when he's stopped?"

"I've found my home, Princess. This is where I belong."

Ilaria could find no subterfuge in his eyes, nor did she hear any in his voice. She found it highly unlikely he was still loyal to King Rith. If he'd truly infiltrated the Sitheen resistance and sought the stones for his king, Rith wouldn't have deemed it necessary to come through the gate himself.

She nodded. "I fear Rith will destroy both worlds. Tell me of Luciar and Sanderis. We encountered them on our way here today." Having been one of King Rith's guards himself, Kaderil would certainly know them.

All eyes sharpened, shooting to Harrison.

"We came upon them on Water Street," Harrison told them. "They claimed to want to protect Ilaria, but when she declined their protection, they tried to grab her. I used fire to imprison them, but never sang the death chant."

Kaderil nodded. "Sanderis is a loyal sort, easily led. Luciar seeks power of his own and curries the king's favor to get it." His gaze swung to Ilaria. "He would see delivering you to King Rith as a great achievement."

"Are there others whose loyalty to Rith would break if they knew what he was?" Ilaria asked.

"If they knew he was a Caller?" Kaderil shook his head. "None that I saw the night they came through, though I didn't see all of them. Most are either intensely loyal to him, or too weak to turn against him regardless of what he is."

So she was well and truly alone. For now, the Sitheen and Kaderil were her only allies. But even they worked at cross-purposes to her.

"Thank you, Kaderil. When there's time, I'd like news of the court and all that's transpired there since the death of the queen."

Kaderil inclined his head. "It would be my pleasure, Princess."

"One thing," she added. "What were my people told of my disappearance?"

Kaderil hesitated. Finally he said, "We were told that you and your mother were both traitors."

"Did they believe that?"

"Some, yes, perhaps. Most, no. But none dared admit it."

That knot of tension eased inside her. "Thank you, Kaderil."

As Kaderil stepped back, Jack pulled something out of his pocket. Even before he opened his palm to reveal the treasure nestled within, she knew he had the draggon stone. Its magic sang within her.

As he opened his hand, Ilaria's eyes drank in the sight of the blue, teardrop-shaped rock that now hung on a silver chain. Fifteen hundred years had passed since she last saw it. Fifteen hundred years since she'd last held it in her hand, and then as the princess, not the rightful queen.

"We rescued you, Princess, because we need your help," Jack said. "We're trusting you because we have to." His tone was calm, but within his words she heard the threat. If she turned on them, betrayed them in any way, she'd become their enemy. And they would destroy her with their rivers of fire, ending her life as they had other Esri lives before hers.

Butterflies fluttered in her stomach, but she held tight to her composure, gaining strength from the warm press of Harrison's hand around hers.

Jack tossed the stone to Harrison, the chain catching the light as it rippled through the air.

Harrison released her and caught the necklace with ease, then opened his palm in front of her. The power of the stone cried out for her, setting the air to quivering around her as it reached for her. Her own need to take it grew to a fever pitch, but she hesitated, all too aware of the armed humans surrounding her. All too afraid of what would happen the first time the stone came into her possession as the rightful vessel for its power.

She sought Kaderil with her gaze, seeking help. "My hair will rise." The sight of an Esri coming into power had always awed and terrified the humans.

"And your eyes will glow like emeralds lit from within," Harrison said calmly beside her, drawing her gaze back to him.

"You know?"

"We know. We're ready for it."

She watched him uncertainly, the stone's energy clawing at her impatiently, calling, demanding. Her hands began to shake, her pulse speeding. She'd been born for this. All her life, she'd waited for this moment. And now that it was upon her, she hesitated. In the proper scheme of things, she should be in the grand temple of the Fair Court, surrounded by her people as she came into her royal power, showered with love and affection and celebration.

Instead she stood among humans—strong and cunning humans who sought to use her power for their own purpose, to seal all the gates between their worlds. A purpose they didn't realize was impossible, for neither world could survive completely cut off from the other. As different as they were, they were two halves of a whole, dependent upon one another in ways neither Esri nor humans had ever understood. Only once, a very long time ago, had one of her ancestors attempted to seal both gates, for in that distant time there had only been two. Just the attempt had rained terrible destruction upon both realms—floods and quakes and storms beyond comprehension. Her ancestor had died in the world's fury. And two gates had become twelve.

No, she could never seal all twelve gates.

But the humans, she feared, would never accept that truth.

With a deep breath, she reached for the stone. The moment the draggon touched her flesh, the mystic energy leaped at her, rushing into her in a thick, wonderful surge.

Strength, well-being, rightness.

As she curled her fingers around the draggon and lifted it from Harrison's palm, the energies raced through her blood, her chest, her mind, at once intense pleasure and perfect calm, filling her to overflowing, bursting from her pores until she could do nothing but fling her head back and ride the storm.

Though her gaze was fixed on the gray clouds above, her mind exploded with swirling eddies of color and life as the energy took root inside her. Deep within her, the stone sang, calling to her, calling to all of Esria, proclaiming her the true queen. With the draggon in the queen's possession, the land would flourish once more. Esria would be whole…if the scourge of Rith could be removed.

In that part of her mind connected to all the Esri, emotions sprang forth as her people responded to the draggon stone's claiming her their rightful monarch.

She felt their shock, surprise, joy. Dismay.

Perhaps a half dozen of those emotions were especially strong. The emotions of the Esri here in the human realm. One sang with joy, a couple felt confusion, several displeasure. A single point of fury burned white hot.

Rith.

But beyond the myriad emotions, she felt something else. Something far closer than the other Esri. A tight core of contained strength and energy pulsing, seeking freedom. She sensed it nearby, practically within reach. Opening her senses and her mind, she reached for it. *There.* Right where...

Her head snapped down, her eyes flying open to stare at the man. The source of that contained, unleashed power.

Harrison.

From the start, she'd felt something within him, the promise of a power she didn't understand. And he felt it, too. She could see the startled look in his eyes, the blend of surprise and awe she herself felt.

Knowledge and awareness flowed between them. Her pulse raced, her skin turning flushed and damp. The power spinning within her bounded as if she were not the only one mesmerized by this man. As if the mystic energies sought to claim him, too.

Why? What was Harrison? What gift did this

human, this Sitheen, possess that the draggon stone recognized?

The connection that formed between them stole the air from her lungs, grabbing her, binding her in a way that went beyond the physical. Her chest tightened, her heart at once contracting and expanding as if it were under assault. She felt compelled, pulled, as if she were tumbling into that piercing gray-green gaze, falling....

With a cold slide of understanding, she realized what was happening. Deep in her mind, a door had unlatched. A door none had ever passed through. None had ever even touched. It was a door she'd known existed within her mind as it did in all Esris, but had expected to never feel. Few ever did.

And with a hard, sinking feeling of disbelief, she knew.

In Harrison Rand, in a *human,* she'd found the man destiny had chosen to be her mate.

Chapter 9

Harrison stared at the strange and amazing sight—Ilaria, her green eyes glowing, her hair twisting above her head—and felt not revulsion, not fear, but a fierce rush of excitement. His blood fizzed as if the fluttering excitement had taken up physical residence in his veins.

Chills raced over his skin, lifting goose bumps on his arms as he watched her skin take on a luminous glow and her eyes fill with rapture.

He'd thought she was beautiful before. Now she took his breath away. Her scent floated to him on a wave of energy—the scent of gardenias… sweeter, richer, more enticing than ever.

Raw power filled the air between them, swirling around them. He couldn't see it, couldn't smell it, yet he could feel it seeping into his skin, tingling through his blood and sinking deep down into his body. A power he recognized on a molecular level, yet had never before experienced.

He felt drawn, as if consumed by an unnatural craving that at once enthralled and disturbed him, as if the energy itself seduced, filling him with a sense of joy, of a *rightness* of such magnitude that he knew he was experiencing one of the most profound moments of his life—Ilaria coming into her power, her ascension to queen.

Everything around him fell away and he was lost in the moment, as if enclosed in a bubble.

A fist of recognition carried down that line of connection between them and the power of the moment trebled. Joy and wonder showed in her face. Answering emotion rushed up inside him as if she poured those feelings into him, and him alone. Inside, he felt his chest begin to ache from the force of her velvet assault.

Passion twisted with the other emotions until his hands shook from the need to touch her, to pull her into his arms and kiss her. In those glowing emerald eyes, he saw an answering need, a hunger to rival his own. Desire flared, heating his blood until he was thick and hard and throbbing from the need to be inside her.

Slowly, the force of the power began to ebb. Little by little, the glow in her eyes faded to a natural brilliance, her hair dropping, as if in slow motion, to settle around her shoulders in a living cloak of pale curls.

But the fire in her eyes burned as her gaze remained tangled with his, her breath as broken as his own, mutual desire pulsating between them.

His hands fisted at his sides as he fought the nearly overwhelming compulsion to take her in his arms and fuse his mouth with hers. If they'd been alone, nothing could have kept him away from her in that moment.

Beneath his feet, the world shifted, righting itself as if in some indefinable way, this was the moment he'd waited for all his life.

No, not this moment.

This woman.

Charlie cleared his throat. "Earth to Harrison."

Harrison struggled back from the precipice,

his body fighting for the freedom to take what was his. *His*.

Good God. *His?* What was he thinking? She was immortal. An Esri princess, soon to be queen. He'd lost his freaking mind.

With a hard, mental yank, he jerked himself free, tilting his face to the sky to stare at the gray clouds overhead as he struggled to regain control.

What in the hell just happened? From the moment he met her, he'd wanted her, yet within the thrall of that power, that need had exploded. All he could think about was touching her, kissing her, making love to her.

But not here. Not in front of his brother and friends.

"Princess?" Kade stepped forward into the circle, a sense of urgency about him that helped Harrison regain control. "We need to do this quickly. Every Esri now knows you're free, and the true queen. Including King Rith."

"What do you mean?" Jack demanded.

"All Esri are connected. We just felt our queen come into her power."

Harrison's gaze shot to Ilaria as she nodded.

Her color was high, roses of pure pink brightening her cheeks, making her even more beautiful, if such a thing was possible.

"I felt the emotions of the race," she told them, her head held high. "Some were joyous, others dismayed. Rith is furious."

"Great," Jack muttered. "Did you know this was going to happen?"

"No," Kade replied.

Ilaria shook her head. "No queen has come into her power in seven thousand years. The last was my mother."

Harrison's gut clenched. Seven *thousand*.

Jack's gaze swung to Kade. "Will King Rith be able to track the princess now?"

"I don't think so, but he can definitely track the stone."

"Should we be calling you the queen now?" Charlie asked.

Ilaria shook her head. "No. Though he seized his power by foul means, Rith rules Esria. The people and the land know I'm the one who should be queen, but Rith still wears the crown. And as long as he does, I remain only a princess."

Kade turned and knelt on one knee before her.

For one uncomfortable moment, Harrison remembered the way the big man had gone up in flame the last time he was touched by one of his own. But Ilaria wouldn't hurt him. He believed that.

"I honor you, my queen," Kade said. "And recognize you as the true sovereign of Esria. However, my fealty belongs to the humans and their cause."

"Thank you, Kaderil. I don't ask for your fealty. It's enough that you fight to stop Rith."

"Will you forgive the death mark upon me?"

"Why do you have it?" Her words were perfunctory, a necessary question rather than a true demand.

"Zander, another of Rith's guards, attempted to kill me and the woman I loved. I killed him first."

Ilaria paused only a moment, as if testing the truth of his words, then with a small nod, stepped forward and lifted her hand.

Around him, the others tensed, but none interfered. If Kade hadn't trusted her, he wouldn't have knelt within Ilaria's reach. And Kade, more than any of them, knew the risk.

Harrison alone watched her calmly. He knew she wouldn't hurt his friends. He *knew* her inside out, he realized, and the last of his wariness dropped away, a thick warmth rushing in to take its place.

Ilaria placed her palm on top of Kade's dark head and closed her eyes. Like before, Harrison felt the power as she called it, though not as strongly as the first time. It raced along the surface of his skin, a flood of energy and pleasure.

He glanced at Charlie. "Do you feel that?"

His brother looked at him quizzically. "Feel what?"

Harrison shook his head. "Nothing." Glancing from Jack to Larsen, he could tell neither of them knew what he was talking about, either.

Less than a minute later, Ilaria lifted her hand, her eyes somber. "It's done."

"Thank you, Princess." Kade stood and backed away.

For a moment, no one moved, then Charlie stepped forward and knelt before her as Kade had.

Harrison watched with a calmness he wouldn't have believed possible even a few hours ago.

Ilaria placed her hand on Charlie's head, her pale lashes sweeping down over flawless ivory cheeks. Once more, he felt the energy, and then it was gone. As Charlie rose and stepped back, Ilaria turned to Harrison, a smile lighting her eyes. Not a smile of mischief, but of thanks. For trusting her.

He nodded, feeling his own eyes crinkle. For so long all he'd wanted was the Esri gone and his world back to normal. Now…the thought of Ilaria disappearing from his life for good made his chest ache. He barely knew her, and had always known her. He'd been waiting for her all his life.

Longing fisted in his chest. His fingers itched to feel the springiness of her soft, ivory curls, to touch her cheek, her lips. To slide down her silken neck and brush the gown from her shoulders, baring her naked breasts to his seeking, desperate hands.

Hell, he was nearly out of control with this need for a woman he had no business wanting. If he were smart, he'd let one of the others guard her now that they were all about to be free of their death marks, then he'd put a healthy bit of distance between them. Maybe then he'd be able to clear his head and regain some much-needed perspective.

When Ilaria was finished forgiving Larsen's and Jack's death marks, the cop held out his hand, palm up. "Thank you, Princess. I'll need the draggon stone back, now."

Ilaria tensed, slowly turning to stone.

Harrison felt his hackles rise in a rush of fierce protectiveness. With bitter control, he slammed that protectiveness to the ground. Jack was only doing what he had to. It didn't matter that Ilaria resented it. And she clearly disapproved.

She lifted her chin, her manner regal. Haughty. "The draggon stone is mine. It stays with me."

Tension rippled through the group. Harrison took a step toward her as the stone's power whispered through him, telling him with a certainty he didn't doubt that the stone was hers. It should never be parted from her. Yet even as his instincts told him she needed to keep it, logic told him otherwise. Keeping the draggon stone would only make her a target. Rith might not be able to wield the full power of the draggon stone, but he was a stone scenter. All Callers were. And the draggon's magical scent would lead him right to Ilaria.

"Princess." Jack's tone held a sharp note of warning, which only served to ignite her temper.

Ilaria slammed her fists onto her hips. "Enough of this foolishness! These stones are Esri, left here *by me* to keep them out of Rith's hands. Now he's found them and I'm taking them back until he can be stopped." She scowled at the lot of them. "*You* clearly can't keep them safe."

Jack's expression hardened, as did the others'. Harrison took another protective step toward her.

Ilaria glanced at him, her eyes sharp and determined, before turning back. "This time, *I* will protect them."

"How?" Charlie asked, the word a question wrapped in steel.

Her chin lifted a fraction higher. "I am the rightful queen of Esria."

Jack looked to Kade.

The big Esri shrugged. "It is said no one can

take the draggon stone from the queen unless she wills it, but I've never heard that of the other stones."

Jack turned back to Ilaria and lifted an eyebrow.

"The stones are mine, human. You lost three to Rith. None of us can afford for you to lose the rest of them."

It was clear she didn't have an answer that would satisfy them. It was equally clear, they were at a standoff if they couldn't take the draggon stone from her by force.

"Every second that stone stays unprotected, King Rith draws closer," Charlie said quietly.

Jack held out his hand, his eyes hard as flint. "Give me the draggon stone, Princess."

"Do you have any idea what will happen if Rith gets all of the stones?" she asked, her voice as hard as it was stark.

"We've some idea." Jack lifted the flame-thrower to rest against his shoulder, pointed at the sky.

Harrison saw the shudder go through Ilaria and knew she understood the implied threat. But she didn't back down. His admiration for her grew even as his concern propelled him forward.

"Ilaria." He moved between her and Jack, facing her. Cupping her shoulders, electricity arced between them, though whether echoes of her power or pure desire, he didn't know. Heaven help him, he felt the desire like a rush of heat.

Struggling against the pull of her, he concentrated on what he had to say, what he had to know. "Does the draggon stone give you strength you didn't have, the power to protect yourself from Rith and his minions?"

Her jaw tightened, but she shook her head. "I don't think so, no. The queen's power has always been more of a nourishing nature than militaristic. Through the draggon stone, the land is renewed and flourishes. As do the people."

Harrison's hands tightened on her shoulders. "Then listen to me. That pair, Luciar and Sanderis, would have captured you earlier. If I hadn't been there, it would be King Rith you'd be facing right now, not us. If you insist on keeping the draggon stone, there will be nowhere you can hide. He'll find you, you know that."

"Then I'll help act as the bait."

His grip on her tightened. "No. I won't let you risk your life like that. You're too important." *To me.*

The thought shook him and he shoved it away. It wasn't like she'd ever stay here. She had a world to rule, and it wasn't his.

"Work with us, Ilaria." His hands softened, caressing her tense shoulders. "We'll catch him, but we have to keep you safe. The only way to do that is to separate you from the stones until we stop him."

He read clearly in her eyes the battle waging inside her. At least she hadn't responded with another unequivocal *no*.

Larsen's clear voice filled the pregnant silence. "If we're having this much trouble getting the draggon stone away from her now, why do we think she'll seal the gates and leave it behind?"

No one answered. No one had an answer.

Ilaria's gaze tore loose of his and dropped. For long seconds, she was silent, staring at the ground, her body as tense as steel cable. Beneath his hands he felt her shoulders rise on a bitter sigh, then fall with the draining of the tension. Finally, her pale lashes swept up again, her eyes filled with a desperate determination that tore at his soul.

She glanced beyond him and he released her, turning to stand beside her as she faced Larsen and the others.

"What I want doesn't matter." Her voice rang clear and true. "All that matters is that Rith, or any Caller who comes after him, never gets his hands on all seven stones." She lifted her fingers to her eyes, pressing them against her closed lids. When she dropped her hands, her eyes were dark with frustration and bitter resignation.

Slowly, she turned to him. "Take the draggon stone, Harrison. I don't think I can make myself give it to you."

He remembered the rightness he'd felt as she first touched that stone and suspected his innate reluctance to part them again was only a shadow of her own.

Watching her, he reached for the silver chain where it kissed her collarbone. As he slid his fingers beneath the cool metal, electricity jumped in a tingling rush, up his arms, spreading through his body. His jaw tightened and he lifted the chain over her head, careful not to touch the stone, then handed it to Jack.

"Thank you, Princess." Jack pocketed the ancient, mystic necklace.

Harrison turned and stood beside her. When she shuddered and crossed her arms over her chest, he couldn't stand it another minute. He curved his arm across her shoulders and pulled her against him.

She stiffened. Belatedly, he realized he'd probably offended her. He might have sensed her need for comfort, but that didn't mean she'd welcome the reminder…or the public display. But as he started to release her again, she leaned into him, just a little.

"Don't go," she said softly.

Both Larsen and Jack watched him, clearly surprised. Charlie's eyes gleamed, but he remained silent. Kade revealed no emotion at all, but he rarely did.

Ilaria lifted her chin and met the others' gazes, regal even within the curve of his arm. "Rith will follow the scent of the stone. He'll find it wherever you hide it, now."

Jack nodded. "We have a way to keep him from finding it."

Harrison knew what they had planned, because they'd done it before. They'd tuck it in a lead-lined box, tie the box to the bottom of a boat, then move the boat. The scent might lead King Rith to the water, but with any luck, he lose track of it there.

"We have two missions, now," Jack said, addressing the small group. "One is to set up a trap for King Rith at...the other location. We'll be waiting when he comes to get his stones." He looked at Kade. "If we sing the death chant for him while he's holding the stones, what will happen to them?"

"Nothing. Unless I'm mistaken, none of the seven can be destroyed by the death chant." He looked to Ilaria for confirmation.

"You're not mistaken. They'll remain where the holder last stood."

Jack nodded. "That's what I was counting on. Capture Esri wherever possible and avoid death marks at all costs…until we take down King Rith. Every time we retrieve the draggon stone to remove them, we risk King Rith's finding it." His gaze met Harrison's, a question in his eyes. "The second mission is to protect the princess. You want to keep that one?"

His logical side told him to say no. To place her in someone else's hands. She was too tempting, and affected him in ways that were too disturbing. But his need to keep her close had nothing to do with logic. It was primitive. Protective.

"She stays with me."

Ilaria melted against him, just a little, telling him without words of her approval.

Jack stepped forward and shook his hand. "Good luck. We'll contact you as soon as we have something to report." Pulling away, he turned to the others. "Okay, let's move."

Harrison released Ilaria's shoulders and once more took her hand. As Jack, Larsen and Kade started walking, Charlie came over to them, tossing Harrison a small set of keys. His mouth kicked up on one side, a knowing look on his face. "In case you want to try to get to my apartment."

Harrison snorted, but didn't deny Charlie's assumption that he couldn't wait to get Ilaria somewhere private. Preferably with a bed. "Thanks."

Charlie nodded toward the direction the others were walking. "There's more than one boat down there." Bolling Air Force Base, the location of the other three green stones, was just down the river from Ft. McNair. The others would be heading there by boat. "You might want to do the same. Or ask for a car at the gate. The commanding officer is under orders to give us anything we need."

Harrison shook hands with his brother. "Watch your back, Charlie."

"You, too, bro." Charlie smiled the cocky smile Harrison knew so well, but his eyes said what they never put into words. *I love you, brother.* Harrison nodded, knowing his own eyes replied in kind.

As Charlie walked off, Harrison turned to Ilaria. To tell her… To ask her… He couldn't remember. She met his gaze and all thoughts flew from his head. Everything but the need to touch her, to pull her into his arms.

He released her hand to brush the hair back from her face.

"Ilaria."

"Kiss me, Harrison."

It was neither the time nor the place, but he couldn't stand being separate from her another moment. With a stunning loss of control, he hauled her against him, covering her mouth with his in a kiss of such blazing hunger he half expected to burst into flames. One hand dove into her hair, the other curved around her waist, hauling her hips against that part of his anatomy that desperately sought release within her.

She moaned low in her throat, looping her arms around his neck as she pressed herself hard against him and opened her mouth, her tongue sweeping out to welcome his.

She tasted of goodness and tears and warm, willing woman. Beneath his hand, her back curved, strong and sure, and her small head nestled perfectly in his palm.

Her scent, gardenias and lush, passion-filled nights, intoxicated him.

He kissed her desperately and she kissed him

back with equal fierceness. Need and aggression, desire and sweetness. He drank of her lips, plundering her mouth, holding her tight against him. If only he could keep her like this, in his arms, forever.

The kiss blazed red-hot for only moments, before he remembered where they were and wrenched back control. With Herculean effort, he pulled back, though his arms refused to listen when he ordered them to let her go.

"I want you," he said against her temple. "I can't deny it. But this isn't the time." Looking up, he saw no fewer than six soldiers watching. "And it's definitely not the place."

Just hours ago those soldiers had lost friends and brothers-in-arms to the Esri bastards. Dozens dead. Watching him kiss an Esri must make them feel like pounding the life out of him. Out of both of them.

And he couldn't blame them. Look at all Stephie had suffered at the hands of the invaders.

No, at the hands of one invader. Baleris.

Not Ilaria. Never Ilaria.

He looked down at her, at her pink, kiss-swollen lips, at the heat and shadows in her eyes. Even as he watched, her expression hardened with determination.

"We need to go," she said, pulling away from him.

"I agree. We'll take a boat and get out of D.C. for a while."

"No. I'm not leaving the city."

"Ilaria… King Rith is hunting you now. I can't keep you safe here."

"I'm not asking you to keep me safe. When I came into my queenship, every Esri felt it. In return, I felt their emotions, individual entities. Most, from a distance, back in Esria. A handful, those here, I felt sharply. Most of the latter were surprised and dismayed. Kade felt relief. One, Rith I presume, was furious. And one, just one, felt true joy."

His head turned slightly, his gaze never leaving her face. "Who?"

"I don't know. Those among the royal guard who'd been openly loyal to me were all trapped in the Forest of Nightmares with me."

"But you think there's another, one of the

guards here, who's glad you've claimed the drag-gon stone."

"Yes. I felt relief and devotion twined with that joy. I don't know who he is, but I must find him."

Harrison's jaw tightened as he realized what she was saying. "We're not hunting an Esri."

"I can't just hide. My world is in as much dan-ger from Rith's power as yours."

Tension wove through the muscles of his neck and shoulders as he remembered all too well their last encounter with King Rith's men. What if they'd succeeded in getting him pounded to a pulp? What if they caught her? Rith would never let her return to Esria alive.

"Ilaria, think about this. Whoever your man is, he's almost certainly with King Rith, chasing those stones. It's too dangerous to go anywhere near them, any of them."

"If I can find him, if I can catch his attention without the others knowing, I might be able to convince him to help me. To help us both."

"How will you be able to tell which one is loyal?"

"The same way I was able to feel Kaderil's...

Kade's...satisfaction when I touched the stone. He was close enough that I could tell his emotion distinctly. I believe that will happen with all the Esri, now. Though I can't be certain." She shrugged. "I've never been queen before."

"Clearly your mother didn't possess the same talent or she'd have known she had traitors in her midst."

"Yes, I was thinking the same. Every Esri's gifts are different."

"I still don't like the idea of you getting near them. You've said yourself that only one is likely to be truly loyal. The odds of finding him without being caught by one of the others are poor, Ilaria. You must know that. If they catch you..."

Emerald eyes flashed from beneath pale lashes, a small, determined smile tugging at one corner of her mouth. "You'll help make sure they don't."

He wanted to deny her. Yesterday he would have—he'd have cuffed her and dragged her where he wanted her to go. But things had changed. *He'd* changed. The hatred that had ridden him from the moment Baleris touched Stephie still burned like a live coal in his gut.

But that hatred no longer had anything to do with Ilaria. And if she *could* turn one of King Rith's men to their side it might just give them the advantage they needed to win.

Within those green eyes bright with resolve he saw a need he understood all too well, the need to *do* something, to wrench back control in some way. She was a natural leader. He sensed that. She was used to taking control, as was he, used to acting as she saw fit.

It must have been hell on her to have been imprisoned for three hundred years while her mother was killed and her kingdom stolen by an evil man. And now that she was free and finally able to fight this villain, she was forced to suffer the indignity of mortals tying her up, trying to control her every move.

He'd thought her a goddess as she'd come into her power. What he saw now was a warrior queen. Tying her up again, forcing her to submit to his protection, would be cruel. As much as his own nature craved control, it was time they worked together.

With a sigh, he looked at her critically. Her hair

no longer flew above her head, her eyes no longer glowed, but there was little *normal* about this woman. She shone like a rare diamond among the mundane. If their pursuers were human, glamour would have done the trick, but they weren't.

"You need a disguise. At least a change of clothes."

"My gown is made of a material that protects me from the vast changes in temperature of your world. I need it."

He nodded. "Fair enough. But right now, you're a beacon. You stand out too much. If I can find you something to cover your gown and hair, will you wear it?"

Her nose wrinkled and he found himself almost smiling. "It depends."

"Let's give it a try then." With his head he motioned her to follow him. They crossed the perimeter road to where one of the soldiers stood guard and he told the man what he needed. The soldiers might hate him for consorting with the enemy, but they'd been ordered to give him whatever he wanted and the man radioed in the request without comment. A few minutes later another came running with a drab olive poncho. Perfect.

Ilaria eyed the waterproof nylon with distaste, but allowed him to slide it over her head. He stepped back and met her put-upon look with a smile.

"Better," he said, then closed the distance between them and gathered her thick length of curly hair back from her lovely face, winding the silken softness into an unbound rope, which he pushed down inside the rain gear. The ever-present desire leaped all over again and it was all he could do to not pull her back into his arms for another mind-blowing kiss.

With a will of iron, he released her hair and lifted the hood to obscure her pale beauty.

"I can't see anything but what's right in front of me," she complained.

"True, but if you keep your hood up and your hands tucked inside, no Esri is likely to notice you."

She reached up and pushed back the hood. "I don't like it. Take it off."

Loosely grabbing the front of the poncho, he pulled her close until her scent surrounded him and he was staring into her stubborn face. "Right now, if I start pulling clothes off you, I'm not likely to stop."

She sucked in a breath, her nostrils flaring as her chest rose. "I want that. I want you."

He released the poncho and cupped her jaw, his fingertips warming with the heat of the awareness that sizzled between them. "If I'm taking you back to the streets of D.C., you have to be covered. So it's your choice. We take a boat and get out of here, or you wear the poncho and we hunt your Esri."

In her eyes he watched her stubbornness battle her need to win the bigger war. With a disgruntled twist of her lips, she pulled the hood up over her hair and he knew it was done.

"Let's go," she said briskly and turned toward the gate.

With a nod, Harrison fell into step beside her. Deliberately hunting for a single Esri when the whole lot might be seeking to destroy them both was the most dangerous thing they could do. But he understood her need to do it.

He just prayed this wasn't a decision he lived to regret.

Chapter 10

With the royal power of the draggon stone pumping through her veins, Ilaria felt alive as she never had before. Every sense felt keener, sharper—the feel of the chilly air against her face, the piercing sound of distant sirens. And the smell of smoke… that ever-present reminder that fires still smoldered, ready to burst into flame all over again.

She pressed closer to Harrison, concentrating on the luscious scent of his warm skin as they passed through the gate of Ft. McNair and made their way through the adjoining neighborhood, traveling along residential streets teeming with the confused, the distraught, the injured.

Her life was out of control. As it had been for a long time. Although she'd come into her queen's power, she was not the queen and never would be if Rith got his way. To complicate matters more, after all these centuries she'd found the one male destined to be her mate. And he was human.

She suspected Harrison was beginning to sense the connection between them, too, though he was possibly even less happy about it than she was. If the situation were different—if he were Esri—she'd be thrilled. In so many ways, she saw goodness in him and a rare and wonderful combination of strength and gentleness. The way he'd trusted her when Luciar and Sanderis approached, the way he'd attacked them when they'd moved against her. The way he'd stood at her back as his own people threatened her. Perhaps he hadn't backed her as much as she'd wanted—he hadn't demanded they let her keep the draggon stone—but she'd heard the truth in his words, that he'd feared the stone would endanger her. He'd done it to protect her.

How odd to think that she, the rightful queen of Esria, might need protecting against mere humans. But she had. And she'd known a strange and wonderful certainty that Harrison wouldn't let anything happen to her. It disturbed her how much pleasure that fact brought her. His putting her safety before his own should make her feel weak, even vulnerable. But it didn't. She felt… treasured.

Very disturbing.

The day was cold and overcast, a chill wind blowing. Her gown kept her warm, but the air bit into her cheeks in a way Esrian air never did. Her hands brushed against the stiff, cool fabric of the poncho as she walked, her fingers curling away from the disagreeable feel. But Harrison had insisted she wear it.

She glanced at him, at his strong profile, his cheeks lightly pinkened by the cold wind. A mix of warmth and desire moved through her every time she looked at him and she wished things could be different. Their paths could follow one another's for only a few short days. They would part, then, all too likely as enemies.

She hated that she had to plot against him, but the humans had made it clear they wouldn't trust her with the stones. If she tried to thwart them, they'd consider her an enemy. Harrison wouldn't let them hurt her, she was almost certain, but if any of them knew her true plan—to steal the stones and take them back to Esria—they'd imprison her and try to find another way to seal the gates.

She didn't blame them for wanting the gates closed once and for all, but what they wanted was impossible. Trying to close all twelve gates would not just end in her destruction, but very possibly that of both worlds. The only option for any of them was to destroy the stones of Orisis before Rith called their deadly power.

So she plotted against the humans without any clear plan. She'd hoped that once she earned their trust, they'd freely turn the stones over to her. But she now knew that would never happen.

Her second option was abhorrent—to enchant an army of humans to move against them as Rith had at Ft. McNair. Sitheen would die. Harrison would be devastated, if he survived.

Sweet Esria, there had to be another way.

She was pinning all her hopes on the one man among Rith's guards she sensed was loyal to her, praying he'd be able to give her another option.

Praying he didn't turn against her as Luciar and Sanderis had.

If there was a way to beat Rith without the Sitheen being harmed, she couldn't see it. She kept telling herself it couldn't matter if one or all of the Sitheen died. That no one person was more important than stopping Rith.

And while she knew in her mind it was true, her heart no longer agreed. Harrison had become important to her and she bled at the thought of how he would suffer if any of his friends died.

But worlds would fall if she failed.

"It's going to take days to clean up this mess," Harrison muttered as they made their way through the wreckage. He made a sound deep in his throat. "All this from a single song. Another blackout like the last one, especially during daylight hours, will send this city into a panic from which it might take years to recover. People will be terrified to go near their cars, or any kind of public transportation, terrified to take a bath or shower for fear of drowning, terrified of turning on the stove for fear of setting the house on fire."

He shook his head as if the thought of it was too much to comprehend.

"What do you think they believe happened?" she asked.

"Those in charge know the truth. The rest will probably assume a terrorist attack of some kind. Everyone will hope and pray it's a one-time event. Let's hope they're right."

At the next street, they reached the end of the building and rounded the corner.

Ilaria froze.

Fire. Across the street, flames crawled out of the windows of an apartment building. Her mind blanked. Her heart flew up into her throat.

A firm hand went around her shoulders, ushering her away.

"Ilaria. Angel."

She didn't know how far they'd walked or how long. When she finally came back to herself, she found her back pressed against cool brick, Harrison's hand on her cheek, his eyes deep pools of concern. His thumb caressed her cheek and she felt moisture, belatedly realizing that she was crying.

Her palm flew to her forehead. "I'm all right." But her voice came out soft and thready. "Just give me a minute."

Instead, he pulled her into his arms.

She stiffened, struggling for control. But his arms around her felt too good, too right, and she gave in to the weakness and buried her face against Harrison's neck, her arms sliding around his waist. As she clung to him, his hand stroked her hair.

"Deep breaths, angel."

She did as he asked, forcing herself to breathe fully. Little by little, her racing pulse began to settle, her shaking began to ease.

"That's it." His hand stroked her hair over and over, a firm, yet gentle touch that resonated with strength. When was the last time she'd accepted comfort from another? From almost as far back as she could remember, she'd been the one others looked up to. The princess. The strong one. Yet being held by Harrison felt so right. His strength slowly seeped into her. The warmth of each caress eased the chill that dampened her skin.

"I hate it when this happens," she said quietly

on a deep, shuddering breath. The sound of a scream, followed by the shouted orders of the firefighters punctured the illusion of safety and she knew they hadn't gone far. "Let's get away from here."

"I agree." He curled his arm around her shoulders and led her away from the shouting and the thickening smoke. When they'd walked a few blocks, his hand slid off her shoulder to grasp hers. "This fear of yours…" They passed a group of humans standing on the sidewalk in a close huddle as if seeking warmth. And comfort. "How did Rith ever get you into the center of the Forest of Nightmares?" He squeezed her hand. "You don't have to talk about it. But I'd like to understand."

His voice was so warm, so gentle. As they left the noise of the fire behind them, she found herself telling him.

"There were only three Esri in all of Esria capable of traveling the Forest of Nightmares unmolested. They were the ones who'd invaded the Marceil stronghold at its center centuries before, and enslaved the last of the Marceillian priestesses. From those three Esri, Rith knew of the clearing that would allow prisoners to live, trapped. He ordered them to transfer me and a guard of twenty into that place until I could be trusted to support him. At least that's what he told them. The twenty guards were blindfolded, allowing them to pass with only minimal molestation by the forest. But Rith never intended for me to leave with my mind intact. He'd managed to kill my mother without being implicated. He couldn't overtly kill me, too. So he devised a plan to destroy me in another way."

"Through your fear of fire."

"Through my fears, yes. The forest serves up whatever you fear most. I was tied to a tree in the forest and left there, per Rith's orders. Much, much later I was told how long I was there, but time meant nothing. I was consumed by fire, in everything but fact...for two weeks."

As they crossed a street and started down another block, the cold wind whipped at Ilaria's cheeks, stealing beneath the hood of her poncho to chill her ears.

"When the two weeks were up, one of the three

who could travel the forest took me to the clearing where the others waited. Apparently Rith had ordered the three killed so that none of us could ever escape."

"They didn't kill them, of course," Harrison murmured. "They were your only way out."

"The guards had no choice. All Esri know when another is killed, and at whose hands. Rith had threatened to torture their loved ones if the three did not die."

Harrison steered her off the sidewalk, up a small path to an arbor tucked between two brick apartment buildings where the wind was all but blocked. Then once more, he slid his arms around her waist, holding her loosely as she talked. Anchoring her.

"So they killed them."

Ilaria slid her hands along the hard length of his arms, absorbing his warmth and strength. "Yes. The leader of my personal guard, a man intensely loyal to me, sang the death chant."

"But you didn't kill him for it."

"Of course not. And neither did the others.

Every man there offered to take that death mark to avenge me."

"But you couldn't remove his mark without the draggon stone."

She swallowed. "No." Did he suspect she wouldn't leave it behind? "I can't get them out of the forest, even if I had the stone."

But she would. Somehow, she'd find a way to free those who'd been forced to sacrifice so much for their loyalty to her. For it was only those most loyal to her that Rith had been so keen to incarcerate.

Harrison's hand cupped her head. "How did you recover?"

She looked up, meeting his gentle gaze. "It wasn't easy. It took more than two years before I was even minimally back to normal and decades before I stopped having nightmares every time I closed my eyes." Her expression turned rueful. "I'm still not fully recovered, as you've seen. I doubt I ever will be. I used to love the human realm, despite the fire. Now…" She shook her head.

She wouldn't be returning anytime soon. Even

if she did manage to destroy the stones, she couldn't come back, at least not to D.C., until the Sitheen here were long gone. They were going to hate her.

Especially Harrison.

Moving closer, she wrapped her arms around him and held on tight. The thought of his strength and vibrancy turning to dust twisted painfully inside her as she buried her face against his collarbone, feeling his arms tighten around her. For long moments, they stood there, tight in one another's arms, before she finally pulled back and looked up at him.

"I wish…" So many impossible, confusing things.

Silently, he stroked her cheek. In his eyes, she saw an answering regret, an echoing confusion.

Then he dipped his head and covered her mouth in a kiss at once tender and needy. His warm lips moved slowly at first, sensuously, then with more insistence as the passion rose, spilling over in a gentle torrent.

Ilaria kissed him back with equal intensity, drinking in the feel of his lips against hers, starved for the taste of him. His scent wrapped around her, his warmth enveloped her in a living heat. Their tongues tangled, stroking, caressing.

Slowly, he pulled away, laying a kiss on her cheek, then another on her forehead before finally straightening to look down at her, tenderness in his eyes. "Are you feeling better?"

She gave him a wry smile. "My heart's still racing, but it no longer has much to do with the fire."

An answering smile lit his face and he lifted his hand to stroke her cheek. She'd happily stay like this forever, staring into his eyes. But they had an Esri to find. With regret, Ilaria pulled out of his arms. Hand in hand, they started walking again.

They'd traveled only a few blocks when she felt it, something tugging at her mind. It didn't hurt, yet felt intensely odd, as if someone were knitting inside her skull, weaving threads between her and…her people. Literal, physical threads. *Amazing.* As if she were the center of a great web to which all the threads connected. They were hers. And she theirs.

As she'd felt them when she came into her power, so she felt them now, more and more clearly. Glowing life forces at the end of each of those threads. A few glowing brightly. Two, brightest of all, as if only a short distance away.

She blinked as understanding hit her.

The two Esri were nearby.

She could feel them like pinpoints of heat, but their emotions were hidden. Perhaps her ability to sense their loyalty had already dissipated. If only she could tell if either of these was the one she sought.

Pulling her mind inward, she concentrated on those small flares of heat and realized she could locate them all.

She glanced at Harrison. This newfound ability to sense the whereabouts of the Esri would be of great use to the Sitheen. If she shared it. And perhaps she should. Whatever she could do to strengthen Harrison's trust in her would only help her later.

She hated the subterfuge. If only she could tell him the truth. All of it.

But that was impossible. So she'd tell him what she could, whatever wouldn't hurt her own mission.

He turned to meet her gaze, as if feeling her eyes on him. "What is it?"

"I feel them. All of them."

His gray-green eyes turned as sharp as knife-points. "The Esri?"

"Coming into my power has connected me to them. I feel two nearby."

His body stiffened. "Where?"

"I'm not sure. Not…here. But close."

"How close?"

She shook her head, not sure how to explain. "In my mind, I see them like bright stars in your sky. But I'm too new at this to understand distances yet."

"What about the others?"

"There are five more elsewhere in the city. They've split up into a total of three groups."

He watched her keenly. "How are they moving? As if they're converging on one location, or wandering aimlessly?"

"The latter."

"As if they're searching."

"Yes."

Harrison grunted. "They don't have a clue

where those stones are." He pulled out his phone. A moment later, the faint sound of Charlie's voice drifted to her. "Hey."

"The princess seems to have acquired some kind of locating ability. She can sense where the Esri are, in a general sort of way." He explained what she'd told him. And what he thought it meant.

Charlie swore. "So we're out here twiddling our thumbs for nothing."

"Maybe, maybe not. One or more Esri may have suspected Ilaria would be able to sense their whereabouts now. They may have split up just to throw us off. Ilaria and I are going to try to follow one of the pairs and see where they lead us. If we get lucky, we may stumble upon the king himself."

"I'm not sure that's getting lucky," Charlie drawled. "If I could be sure Rith wasn't going to try for the stones on his own, I'd get your back."

"I don't plan to engage him."

"I'm pretty sure you weren't planning to engage the last pair, either. Just…"

"What?"

"Don't lose sight of your mission, big bro. If they kill the princess, it's all over."

Harrison's gaze swept to her, his eyes unreadable. "They're not going to touch her."

Again, that pause. "Be careful, Harrison."

"You, too." Harrison shoved the phone back into his pocket. "Let's get that sucker." Determination and a hint of a smile lit his eyes.

Ilaria smiled, her chest filling with that wonderful warmth. "I agree. Starting with the two nearby." Turning inward, she sought them out. "That way, I think." She pointed to the left. "I can't be sure."

"Are either of these two the one you're trying to find?"

"I don't know. I feel only life forces now. The emotions have faded."

"Then how are you going to know him?"

"I don't know. I'm hoping I'll be able to tell once we're closer. Trust me. At least, now that I can sense them, we won't be surprised like we were last time."

"At least that's something." He squeezed her hand and headed left, as she'd indicated.

Harrison led the way this time, and she let him, knowing beyond a doubt she didn't want to see that fire again. They'd walked for several blocks when he came to a sudden stop, then pulled her behind the abandoned wreckage of a small blue pickup truck.

"Found them."

She peered around him. Halfway up the block, between another pair of buildings, stood two Esri males in silver tunics. Both were in profile facing a woman with her back pressed to the brick wall.

One Esri she didn't recognize. He'd likely come of age during the past three hundred years. But the other, with his high cheekbones and short-cropped curly white hair, she would know anywhere. Findris. He'd been a royal guard for eons, since long before she was born. As a child, he'd been the only one of the silent guard to wink at her or slip her treats when no one was looking. He'd been kind to her when most of the court, her mother included, ignored her.

Though she hadn't seen him in centuries, since long before her mother's death and her own incarceration, seeing him now squeezed her heart with homesickness for a different time, a different life.

Was he the one whose joy she'd felt? Yes. She felt almost certain he was. But whether that old friendship superseded his loyalty to his king was anyone's guess. She had grave doubts that it would. Findris was a good man, she believed that, but through fair means or foul, Rith appeared to have stirred a powerful loyalty in his guards.

She didn't think Findris would try to hand her over to Rith like Luciar had, but she couldn't be certain.

Either way, she had to know. Because Findris was a stone scenter and in the past, Esri with such a gift were often able to call strong magic from the stones. Nothing compared to a true Caller, like Rith, but enough, perhaps, to open the gates before the full moon.

If it turned out he was loyal to her, Findris could be a powerful ally indeed.

Harrison tensed beside her. "They're going to rape her."

She realized he hadn't seen the woman until

that moment. But even as he said the words, the pair turned away, giving Ilaria a good look at their faces. And their eyes. From this distance, Findris's were indistinct. He wasn't the one who'd taken the woman. No, it was his companion whose eyes still glowed.

"It's already done."

Beside her, Harrison swore low and violently. "Please tell me that bastard isn't the one you're looking for because I'm going to kill him." The line of his jaw had turned hard as granite.

"No, he's not the one I'm looking for, but neither are you going to kill him."

"Is either one King Rith?"

"No."

"Is the other the one you're searching for?"

"No." The lie tripped easily off her tongue. She had to find a way to discover her old friend's loyalty without endangering either him or Harrison. Which meant getting him alone somehow.

Beside her, Harrison's fury throbbed, thick and palpable, and she sensed he was a heartbeat away from attacking the two in retribution. She couldn't blame him. Many among her people held a shocking disregard for human life and few, if any, for a woman's virtue.

Her fingers laced tightly with his. "Calm, my fierce friend. She wasn't harmed."

"She was *raped*."

"He enchanted her, making her feel extreme desire before he touched her. An Esri male cannot take an unready female. She likely felt only pleasure and won't remember any of it."

His gaze swung to her, his eyes burning. "And that's supposed to make it all right?"

Her stomach clenched at the raw anger directed at her and she pulled her hand from his, taking a step away. "No. I'm only saying she wasn't harmed. Not physically, at least. Our ways are not yours, Harrison. If I ever claim the throne, I'll do what I can to change our dealings with the humans."

"If you seal the gates, there won't be any need. No Esri monster will ever be able to reach us again."

His words stung and she turned away. He had a right to his anger and it served as a sharp reminder that although they had developed some kind of errant connection, they were of two peoples, of two worlds. Worlds destined to always be at odds.

She hated to use the word *enemies,* yet perhaps that's what they were and would always be, on some level.

"Ilaria." His voice was soft and apologetic. "I'm sorry. I don't blame you." His hand cupped her shoulder. "None of this is your fault."

The gentle contrition in his tone made her want to weep. She turned slowly toward him, wishing she could give him what he wanted—those gates sealed for eternity so that no human ever had to suffer from Esri enchantment again. But that was the one thing she could never do.

His gaze flicked up and behind her. "They're leaving." His expression tightened. "What now? Let them go and keep searching for the one you're looking for, or follow these two and see where they lead us?"

Ilaria frowned, her own gaze turning to Findris and the other Esri as they started down the sidewalk in the opposite direction, ambling as if they had no destination.

A fluttering of panic gripped her at the sight of her old friend walking away. She had to speak to him alone, to test his loyalty and to discuss her true goal with him. To find out if he could help her.

And how in the two worlds was she going to get away from Harrison long enough to do that?

Her mother had possessed the ability to communicate telepathically when she chose. A gift that was said to have been bestowed upon her by the draggon stone. Mightn't her daughter have been given the same gift?

Ilaria's pulse tripped with a hopeful excitement. There was only one way to find out.

Findris. She called to him, directing her thoughts toward that glow she could almost see in her head, a glow she knew was his.

To her delight and amazement, Findris stopped in his tracks and looked around. Delight quickly turned to fear as Harrison pulled her behind him. She was going to ruin everything! With desperation, she threw a blast of emotion to that warm dot of light in her mind. *Secret, secret, secret.*

She saw the other Esri look at Findris questioningly. Findris waved his hand with quick dismissal and continued forward as if his rightful queen hadn't just spoken in his head.

Her heart pounded, her muscles turning weak. He'd understood. She felt certain of it.

I must speak with you in private. Tonight. Somehow she knew she wasn't communicating in words, but instead conveying meaning. Where could she tell him to meet her? She didn't even know where she'd be.

I'll follow you. No words sounded in her head, but his meaning slid warm and comforting around her mind. *My loyalty is yours.*

She believed him. And yet, if he was still the good man she remembered, why was he among Rith's most trusted?

His thoughts continued to slide through her mind. *Call to me when you're ready and I'll come to you.*

To help her? Or to capture her for his king? Her heart told her the former, yet she'd be a fool not to approach him with a healthy dose of suspicion.

At least she'd get her meeting with him.

Not once had he looked her way, yet she felt

certain he knew exactly where she was. If she asked him to come to her now, he'd move toward her unerringly. All the more reason to get Harrison on another path, before a confrontation occurred that ruined everything and endangered both men.

"I feel him," she lied, attempting to insert the proper note of excitement into her voice. "The one who's loyal." Harrison looked at her with question and she shook her head. "Not one of these. He's in that direction." She motioned back and left, away from Findris.

"I'd rather follow these two."

"You'd rather kill these two."

"True. All right. Let's follow that internal GPS of yours and find this guy."

It took her a moment to process the GPS comment, but quickly realized it was a mild attempt at humor. Together, they crossed the street. Just before they slid around the corner, out of sight of Findris and his companion, she looked back. At that very moment, Findris turned. Their gazes collided. Despite the distance, she felt the flare of his emotion. Elation. Relief.

Loyalty.

Unless she was badly mistaken, Findris would help her if he could. How, she wasn't sure. All she knew was that she had to talk to him without Harrison knowing.

Chapter 11

The cold wind had risen, lifting dead leaves to tumble end over end along the sidewalk where he and Ilaria walked. Harrison felt that same tumbling sensation inside himself, his thoughts and emotions a jumbled, spinning mess. Among them, fury and hatred of the Esri. Good God, he'd watched them walk away from raping a woman. It frustrated him to no end that Ilaria just accepted it. Yet, he'd seen with his own eyes that the woman hadn't seemed to be hurt. And she wouldn't remember. Still, that didn't excuse the fact that she'd been assaulted!

Never had his sense of right and wrong been so confused. Life had been so much simpler when he'd believed all Esri were evil. Ilaria's hand tucked warmly within his, he lifted his free hand to his chest, rubbing at the ache that he'd felt bloom there as he'd watched Ilaria smiling at the little girl she'd carried from the damaged minivan. Or had the ache started earlier, when he and Ilaria had first kissed? Hell, he didn't know. All he knew was it had grown to a full-fledged pain.

She looked tired to him, faint bruises beneath her eyes, shadows within them even though outwardly she appeared to have shaken off the effects of seeing that apartment fire. But though she once more walked with confidence, her expression certain, he sensed her lingering unease. They both knew they'd probably come upon other fires before this day was over. And other Esri. The need to protect her felt like a tight band around his chest.

His gaze moved from one side of the street to the other, passing quickly over the groups of people who watched emergency crews trying to pry two vehicles apart from one another. But his interest wasn't in the humans or the wreckage. He was searching for Esri. He didn't like being out in the open like this. Though he'd convinced

Ilaria to use glamour on the humans and wear a poncho to hide from the Esri, his senses remained on full alert, his muscles tense and ready to protect her from anything…or anyone.

His arms ached with the need to hold her and never let her go. In a matter of weeks, as soon as those gates opened again, she'd be gone. Lost to him forever.

How he would love to spend more time with her, showing her around his city, his world. Simple things. Taking her to a movie. Taking her to meet his kids.

That old pain twisted inside him. *Stephie.* Ilaria would heal her, he had to believe it. Would his daughter look at Ilaria with the same adoration the other little girl had? A real fairy princess. Yeah, she would. He knew she would. Sam would be curious about Ilaria, of course, but unless she knew how to throw a baseball or play video games, she wouldn't hold his interest for long. Stephie would chatter Ilaria's ear off with a thousand questions. And Ilaria would answer every one.

If only things could be different. If only he

could have more time with this remarkable woman. When she'd come into her power, when their gazes had caught, he'd felt those impossibly green eyes pull him headlong into their endless depths. When he was with her, he felt no loneliness. Hell, he hadn't even realized he *was* lonely, not until Ilaria had blown into his life and climbed inside him, creating a glowing warmth that filled him as if embracing him from the inside out. How could he ever be cold with her warm glow pulsing inside his chest?

He glanced at her, at the tension in her lovely face, and just wanted to get her out of here. Someplace safe. They'd head north, in the direction of Adams Morgan and Charlie's apartment. If they hadn't seen any Esri by the time they left the disaster zone, he was finding a cab and getting her off the streets. Maybe then he could breathe freely again.

Who was he kidding? They'd be alone together in an apartment with a bed. He'd be lucky if he remembered to breathe at all.

He needed to keep his hands off her. That was the smartest thing to do, on so many levels. Because he was already too drawn to her. He already wanted her too much, and not just to make love to. Still, that would be a huge mistake. His survival depended on keeping *some* distance between them. The survival of his heart.

He slid his hand beneath her hood, beneath that thick fall of curls, and cupped the back of her neck, feeling the cords of tension beneath his fingers. She melted into his touch with a sigh, her head tilting toward him. Knowing she was immortal, he tended to think of her as indestructible. But she was still a living, breathing being. A woman in need of food and sleep. And safety.

"This isn't working." Ilaria pushed back her hood, her pale hair like the finest ivory silk, framing a face of alabaster perfection.

He sent her a questioning look. "I take it there are no Esri nearby?"

"No. None. I can sense them, but I don't seem to be able to follow them." Her words spoke of disappointment, but her tone was flat. Exhausted.

"Some of them could be in cars or other vehicles." He kneaded the tight cords in her neck. "Why don't we work our way to Charlie's apartment, get some dinner and some sleep? It'll be dark soon and we're both exhausted."

She glanced at him, a warm gleam entering her eyes that told him she was thinking of that damn bed, too. His body heated, despite the cold, hardening.

Screw the future.

Tonight, Ilaria was his.

An hour and a half later, Harrison pushed open the door to Charlie's apartment in Adams Morgan, a pair of white bags in one hand—Chinese food, he called it. But despite the delicious smell, Ilaria's hunger had little to do with food. Apparently, Harrison felt the same. One moment, she was walking into the apartment, Harrison kicking the door closed behind them. The next she was in his arms, his mouth plundering hers, his hands in her hair and sliding over her hips. What happened to their dinner, she didn't know and didn't care.

His hands were at once rough and gentle as he grasped her buttocks and hauled her body tight against his. His hard, thick erection pressed against her abdomen. His warm lips brushed hers as his tongue thrust inside her mouth.

She curved her arms around his waist and held on as his scent, his taste, his barely controlled passion swept her into a storm, a wildness she'd never known. And she *hungered*.

Moving back an inch, she slid her fingers to his shirt and began yanking at the buttons, desperate to feel his flesh beneath her palms, desperate to taste his skin. The passion caught her up, flinging her free until her breaths were short and ragged, her heart pounding an unsteady, jubilant rhythm.

Harrison pulled away, yanked his shirt from his waistband, pulled it off over his head and tossed the garment to the floor. His white undershirt followed a moment later. Ilaria stepped forward, running her hands over the warm, hard planes of his magnificent chest, the light furring of hair tickling her palms.

"You're beautiful," she breathed.

With a low growl, his hands grabbed her hips, his fingers digging into the fabric of her gown and pulling upward, lifting her dress until she felt a draft of cool air against her calves, rising to her knees, then her thighs.

His hands gripped her bare hips. One hand slid to the front, probing between her legs, urging her to widen her stance, which she did gladly. His hand slid fully between, a single finger sliding deep inside of her.

Ilaria moaned, gripping his waist to keep herself standing as that finger thrust deeper, retreated, then thrust deep again.

She pressed her mouth to his chest and his shoulder, moaning with pure pleasure.

"Take off your dress," he said against her hair. "I have to see you, Ilaria. I have to touch you."

His words weakened her knees. She reached behind her, pulling the ties that laced up the back of her dress and hung at the base of her spine.

"Loosen them for me," she said, turning so that her back was to him and pulling her hair over one shoulder to get it out of his way.

She could feel his fingers stroking the flesh of her back as he did as she asked, each brush a teasing whisper of promise. With careful hands, he pushed the fabric over her shoulders until the bodice fell, leaving her gowned only from the waist down.

And then his hands were around her, covering her breasts, his warm fingers grasping her gently, kneading the mounds and plucking at her nipples. His mouth found her shoulder, placing teasing kisses along the slope, sending tiny chills of pure delight rippling down her spine.

Arching back, she thrust her breasts more firmly into his keeping, tilting her head to give him better access to her shoulder and the side of her sensitive neck.

Pleasure ran in rippling waves through her body and down her limbs, creating an inferno of desire like nothing she'd ever known.

Straightening, he tugged at the ties a slight bit more and the gown slipped down over her hips and away, baring her to the chilly air. Before she could turn around, Harrison's hands gripped her waist and lifted her out of the gown, leaving her in nothing but the soft boots she always wore. As he set her on her feet again, he turned her in his grip until she faced him.

His gaze traveled down the length of her body,

lingering on her breasts, her waist, the thatch of hair between her thighs, then down her legs and slowly, so slowly, back up again.

When his gaze finally reached hers, the look in his eyes nearly melted her on the spot. His breaths were labored, his hands shaking where he held her. With a low rumble in his chest, he pulled her against him and kissed her fiercely, one hand holding the base of her head as he walked her back until she felt the cool plasterboard of the wall behind her.

His other hand slid around the back of her thigh and pulled her leg up, her knee against his hip as he ground his fabric-clad erection against her, rubbing her in exactly the right spot.

"Harrison," she gasped against his mouth, sliding her hands up his bare chest. "I need you inside me."

One hand pulled off her boots while the fingers of the other slid behind her, between her legs, inside her. As two fingers thrust deep, she flung her head back, banging it against the wall and not caring. His mouth dove for her throat, his lips suckling the curve of her neck. Her fingers dove into his hair, cradling him against her, holding on as pleasure skated through her body, as pressure built between her legs.

"Harrison."

His mouth moved, raining kisses madly along her shoulder like a man possessed. His passion fueled her own, every touch of his mouth sending the fury higher.

While his fingers worked her from the inside, his lips traveled up the sensitive curve of her neck, his teeth nipping at her ear.

With a shuddering sigh, he released her suddenly, lowering her leg. With quick, deft movements, he removed her other boot then pulled back, his hands on his belt, his hot eyes melding with hers.

"I have to feel you against me. All of me."

"Yes."

He discarded his own clothes, pushing the pants down lean hips, revealing a pair of tight, white underwear that molded his man's body, imprisoning it.

With delight, she watched that thick, hard length spring forth as he pushed the underwear down, too. He was as ready for her as she was for him.

Before she could reach for him, he lifted her into his arms, thrilling her with a strength no full-blooded Esri male possessed. Striding across the apartment, he shouldered his way through one of the doors, then stopped abruptly.

Ilaria's gaze swept the room. A bed, a desk and a chest of drawers, just like the hotel rooms she'd seen. But unlike the hotel rooms, this one possessed nothing more. No pictures upon the walls, no curtains at the windows. No linens upon the mattress.

Harrison's grip on her tightened and she could feel his frustration.

"Nothing like having to make the bed to kill the mood."

Ilaria lifted her hand, making him look at her. "I don't need a bed. The floor is fine. Or the sofa. Or standing against the wall. I don't need comfort or finery." She ran her thumb along his firm, full bottom lip. "All I need is you."

"I'm not making love to you on the floor. Not if there's an option."

"Because I'm a princess?"

He smiled, a sweet, quick flash that illuminated his eyes. "Because I want it to be perfect for you."

Inside her chest something soft set up a deep, pulsing ache. A fullness squeezed her heart until she could barely breathe.

He turned and carried her to the sofa in the living room. Laying her down with gentle care, he sat beside her, his gaze moving over her face and body like a heated caress.

She drank in the sight of his broad shoulders and muscular chest and arms, his narrow waist and his full, thick erection. "You're the finest-looking male I've ever seen, Harrison." She slid her hand over his rock-hard thigh. "Come to me."

An intriguing playfulness lit his eyes. "Oh, I intend to, angel. I intend to."

Ilaria smiled, delighted with the man hovering over her. But instead of covering her with his body, as she wished, he moved to kneel on the floor beside her, then dipped his head to take her breast deeply into his mouth. She cried out at the exquisite feel of his tongue on her sensitive flesh, moaning as his hand slid up her thigh, parting her, then playing in the damp folds of her need.

As her hips rocked, she gripped his head, holding him close and reveling in the sweet assault of his lips and mouth, and those clever, clever fingers.

With her own hand, she reached for him, her fingers trailing across his thigh before finding the part of him she sought. As her hand closed around the thick length of his erection, he groaned, his mouth growing rougher, hotter. In her hand, he was the softest down and the hardest granite. And her body wept to feel the full length of him inside her.

Never could she remember being so desperate for a joining. Over the long years of her life, she'd known many, many men. Yet never had she felt anything like this excitement, like this man.

She watched as he showered one of her breasts with attention, then moved to give its twin equal time, equal pleasure. Lifting her hand to his hair, she delighted in the feel of the short, soft strands, tracing her fingers across the curve of his solid head to the strong, corded muscles of his neck.

He lifted his head to peer at her with a smoldering gaze before pressing a kiss to the valley between her breasts before his lips began a slow, downward descent, grazing her belly button before traveling lower.

Heat built inside her as she understood where he was going, what he had in mind. She lost her grip on him as he moved down her body, then caught her breath in anticipation as he slid his hands beneath her hips and lifted her, draping her legs over his shoulders as he raised her hot core to his mouth.

His tongue brushed against that tight knot of sensation and she cried out with pure pleasure. Over and over he licked her, sipped at her, teased her with his lips and tongue until the pressure built, twisting tighter and tighter and finally snapping in a shower of brilliant, pulsing stars. Her breaths became gasps, turning to tiny moans as the pleasure became so intense it straddled the line of pain.

At the very moment the words *too much* formed in her head, he pulled back, as if he knew. He wiped his mouth with the back of his hand and stared down at her, his eyes gleaming with hot satisfaction.

From somewhere she found the strength to lift her arms to him. "Come to me."

And, finally, he did. He covered her, settling himself within the cradle of her thighs. Capturing her gaze with his, he slid inside her with a single perfect thrust, filling her more fully than she'd ever been filled, taking her body and soul.

Sweet Esria, she was falling in love with him. She'd known this would happen. She'd feared…

Their gazes clung as he moved inside her, their bodies joined in the most fundamental of ways. Her heart pounded with the perfection of their joining, and with the ripping knowledge that they might never be together like this again. Tears blurred her vision and she reached for him, pulling him down to kiss her so he wouldn't see. And he did kiss her, tenderly. Thoroughly. Passionately.

She met him, thrust for thrust, as they drove together toward that last, final, brilliant release. It crashed over her in a beautiful violence. Deep inside her, the walls crumbled, her heart opened, overflowing with love and tenderness for this intense, wonderful man.

And her tears ran freely.

Harrison collapsed on top of her, sparing her the bulk of his weight with his forearms, but his head dropped, his cheek pressing against hers.

"You're crying," he said, the soft dismay in his voice a tender caress.

"I'm a woman," she said simply. She couldn't explain. Indeed, she didn't want him to look into her eyes, afraid he'd see the truth—that she loved him. That she was leaving him. Betraying his trust.

After a few moments, he rose and she sat up, brushing away the errant tears.

His hand tangled gently in her hair. "I was going to switch places with you. Let you lie on top." Her stomach growled and tenderness filled his eyes. "How about I feed you first?"

Her heart swelled and clutched, misery a living thing inside her. For the first time in her long, long life, she'd become one with another and now her heart broke at the prospect of leaving. In a strange way, she felt more alone than she ever had before. Because finally, she knew what true connection felt like.

More than anything, she wanted to stay here in his arms. But her wishes were of no account. Not when so many lives hung in the balance. And she and Harrison had never had a future. She'd always known that.

Findris awaited her call. The moment Harrison was fully asleep, she'd escape him, possibly never to return. Whatever relationship had begun to spring up between them would be shattered.

In destroying Harrison's trust, she would be destroying the finest thing she'd ever known. But the safety and survival of two worlds mattered more than the breaking of her heart.

Chapter 12

Harrison took Ilaria's hand and helped her to her feet, watching her rise before him like a marble goddess. She was glorious, her body slender yet ripe with curves, her skin alabaster perfection except for the places he'd marked her during their lovemaking—her breasts softly reddened from his mouth, her lips swollen from his kisses.

He'd known all the reasons he shouldn't have touched her—that she was Esri, *other,* that she'd soon be out of his life forever, that falling for this woman felt like a betrayal of his daughter and all she'd suffered at Esri hands—but in the end he couldn't fight the fact that he'd needed Ilaria...to kiss her, to touch her, to make love to her, and the experience had been a hundred times more exciting, a thousand times more profound than any lovemaking he'd experienced with anyone else.

Including his wife. Ex-wife, now.

Guilt kicked at him for that thought, a guilt that he'd never felt what he should have for Gwen. She'd ultimately realized it and refused to take what little he could give. He'd thought she was being unreasonable and asking too much of him, but he was beginning to understand just how little his mind and body had been engaged in their relationship, despite his commitment to his marriage.

Now, he'd found a woman who moved him, body and soul, and she could never be his. Life was a bitch.

He grabbed his shirt off the floor and held it up for Ilaria. "Would you like to wear this for now, and to sleep in, or do you want your dress?"

She hesitated, then gave him a small smile that didn't quite reach her eyes. "I'll wear my dress. I'm used to sleeping in it."

He helped her into it, then led her to the dining table, where he'd ditched dinner in his haste to get her into his arms. Neither spoke, each reeling, he suspected, from the magnitude of what had passed between them. The aftershocks were still sending lightning arcing through his blood. The thought that, when this was over, once she'd sealed those gates, he'd never see her again, was almost enough to drive him to his knees.

He should be elated at the prospect that his life might actually get back to normal. That's all he'd wanted from the moment the Esri first found their way back into this world. Yet the thought of it brought no relief now, only the dull ache of loneliness. How barren his life had become, without him even realizing it. How much worse it would be without Ilaria.

"What do we need?" she asked over her shoulder. "Plates? Silverware?"

Harrison pulled in a deep, steadying breath and let it out slowly. "God only knows what we'll find. Charlie's kitchen is not what you'd call well-stocked." Until the Esri invasion, his brother had spent most of his time on the road, working one secret ops mission or another.

Harrison rifled through the mostly empty cupboards until he found a pair of chipped plates, a handful of silverware and a couple of paper towel squares that would have to serve as napkins. Setting them on the counter that separated the kitchen from the rest of the apartment, he pulled open the refrigerator. Empty, as he'd expected it would be, but for a couple of take-out cartons that no doubt contained molding food, a bag of fuzzy grapes and a lone can of Budweiser.

"Water it is." He grabbed a couple of mismatched glasses from the cupboard, smirking as SpongeBob SquarePants grinned at him from one and Mr. Spock stared from the other. This place needed a woman's touch and attention, no doubt about it. Then again, if he remembered correctly, Tarrys had a fondness for all things Washington Redskins. The glassware selection might not improve much after they were married.

He filled the glasses with tap water and joined Ilaria at the table, watching as she unpacked the bag, opening each take-out container carefully and sniffing.

Her eyes lit with interest and pleasure. "Human food is so wonderfully varied and complex."

"I guarantee you've never had anything like

this. Not unless one of your gates opens somewhere in China."

She gave him a bemused look. "I don't know where most of the gates opened. I only ever used two of them until that last time when I came here, and the names the humans used to describe their villages were of little consequence to me. The human realm was the human realm."

Harrison picked up one of the containers of rice. "Mind if I serve you?"

That intriguing mouth kicked up. "Not at all."

He started with fried rice, then added sesame chicken and a spring roll with duck sauce. His favorite.

As he served himself, Ilaria tried the food. "Incredible." Her eyes sparkled, that wide mouth tipped up, opening, closing, her tongue darting out to lick her lips, and he couldn't stop watching her.

After what could have been a minute, or an hour, he tore his gaze away and finished serving himself. "What did you eat in the forest?"

"In Esria, the land provides food and water to the Esri. We've only to ask. We don't farm as you do, or raise animals for milk or eggs. We eat off the land much as your earliest ancestors did— hunting wild game and eating the fruits and nuts from the trees, though instead of walking up to a fruit-laden tree and picking what we desire, as you can in this world, we must ask the tree to provide the fruit. There are dozens of fruit and nut-bearing trees in Esria, but in the Forest of Nightmares we were limited to the few trees at the edges of that small, safe clearing. And much to our eternal frustration, only two bore sustenance—a colin fruit tree and one that provided bejue nuts."

"So that's all you ate for three hundred years?"

"Occasionally a wild animal would scamper across our clearing and we'd have meat. If we were quick enough. Otherwise it was colin fruit and bejue nuts." She made a face. "I never want to see either again."

Three hundred years.

The anger at King Rith that rose in him this time was all on Ilaria's behalf, a fury over the fact that he'd trapped this pale jewel of a woman and locked her away for the equivalent of four human lifetimes. And now that she was free, Rith would try to destroy her.

"If we grow thirsty," she continued, "or wish to bathe, a pond appears if we ask, then disappears within the hour."

"That sounds bizarre."

Her mouth tilted up. "Only because you're not used to it." In her eyes gleamed a knowledge and a wisdom that reminded him again that she was no twenty-five-year-old, despite her youthful appearance.

When they'd finished eating, Harrison cleaned up, then found sheets and made the bed. Taking Ilaria's hand, he pulled her down with him, covering them with the sheet and blanket. He wrapped his arm around her and pulled her close until they were spooned together tightly.

As they lay like that, her warm flesh pressed against his own, he felt…grounded…centered, as if, clichés aside, he'd found his other half. Content, he let exhaustion sweep him into sleep.

Sometime later he woke to the feel of Ilaria slipping out of his arms. He tightened his grip, pulling her against him, but she patted his hand.

"Bathroom," she said softly, placing a soft kiss on his shoulder, a kiss that warmed his heart.

He let her go and sank back into his dreams.

Something woke him a second time, though he couldn't be sure what. The click of the front door?

He bolted upright, the thought wrenching him from sleep. In the light from the street that seeped in between the window blinds he saw the bed beside him was empty.

His memory caught up with his instincts and his heart began to slow its frantic pace. Ilaria had gotten up to go to the bathroom. The sound he'd heard was her moving around the apartment somewhere.

But some deeper instinct had him sliding from the bed without sound. No lights had been turned on, though enough light filtered in from the street below that he didn't really need any. The bathroom door was open. And dark.

And there was no sign of his bedmate, no sound but his own. "Ilaria?"

He walked into the living room and turned on the light, but he was alone. His heart began to race as he looked at the spot where he'd removed her boots. They were gone.

Dammit, he *had* heard the click of the door. He lunged for it now, yanking it open just in time to see the elevator door swish closed on a flash of green.

She'd left him.

His mind reeled even as he whirled and grabbed his shirt where it still hung over the back of the sofa. His thoughts spun. Why? Had she been waiting for him to let his guard down all along and had simply taken advantage when he had? The thought twisted like cold steel. His mind shied from the thought that he'd been wrong about her. That she wasn't who she'd pretended to be and had played him all along as he'd fool-ishly, foolishly fallen for her.

He grabbed his pants and shoved his bare feet into his shoes, not bothering to tie them, then grabbed his coat and flew from the apartment, running for the stairs. As he started down the sec-ond flight, one of his shoes slipped off his foot. He shoved it back on and tied it, but as he yanked the laces tight on the second, one lace snapped.

Dammit. Two flights later, that shoe, too, came off and he left it behind. Charlie's shoes would fit him, if he'd left a spare pair in the closet, but there was no time to go back and search.

Reaching the ground floor, he shoved through the door into the lobby to find the elevator door standing open and empty. Ilaria was already gone.

He pushed through the front door and into a shower of falling snow. The frigid air lashed at his face, the cement freezing his bare foot. But all that mattered was finding Ilaria.

Before King Rith did.

He searched in every direction, seeking another flash of emerald, but the streets and sidewalks were still busy, bundled pedestrians hampering his view. The hour couldn't be late yet. Nine, maybe ten o'clock?

His instincts sent him left and he followed without question. At the corner, he turned just in time to glimpse a flash of bright green against the snowy background two blocks up, and he took off running, ignoring the wind whipping at his face and the snow quickly freezing his foot.

He dashed across the side street, darting around a car as the driver honked, then down the second block to the corner where he'd seen Ilaria disappear. But as he rounded the corner, he pulled up, staring at the empty sidewalk. Ilaria was nowhere in sight.

Falling snow stung his hands and cheeks, dropping into the vee of his shirt, where he'd never bothered to zip the jacket. Icy knives plunged into his foot, the cold seeping into his blood, his mind.

His heart.

Ilaria stood in the swirling snow as Findris knelt before her, his pale curls cut close to his head, his skin as white as the snow falling around them. He watched her with eyes the dark rich green of jade. Eyes that shone with affection. And joy.

"This is a great day, Princess Ilaria. For too long we've prayed for a miracle that would free you. Esria needs you, my true queen. Desperately, we need you."

She could feel his emotion, his sincerity, as

clearly as she could see it in his achingly familiar face.

"Rise, old friend." She watched him stand, then asked the question that weighed heavy on her heart. "Why do you serve him, Findris? Why do you call Rith king? Why does he trust you so?"

His face tightened, his mouth twisting wryly. "A bit of preemptive maneuvering on my part, Princess. When King Rith first came into power, he sought out the stone scenters. In those early days, few willingly supported him and the first ones he asked to join him refused. He made an example of them. Those who'd refused soon found the people they cared for beaten and their lands and possessions seized. It became clear that to deny Rith was to suffer. I'm not proud of myself, Princess, but there was no fighting him. Before he could demand my allegiance, I gave it and have acted the loyal man since, praying for the day I could find a way to release you."

"And now? Who holds your allegiance?"

"You, my queen. My allegiance has been yours since the day your mother died."

In his eyes she found nothing but raw truth.

And while she could no longer read his emotions as she had when she first touched the draggon stone, in her heart she felt his sincerity. The last of her doubts melted away.

She smiled. "I'm glad, Findris, for I desperately need your help." At least there was one among her own, one not trapped within the Forest of Nightmares, she could still call friend.

"If I'd known a way to free you from that prison, I'd have done it long, long ago. Many tried, did you know that? Many, many of us sought entrance to that forest over the years, hoping another among us possessed the ability to pass unmolested, but no one ever succeeded. Now that you're free, I'll fight to put you on the throne. It's where you belong. Where you've always belonged." His expression turned grim. "He's a Caller."

"Yes. I've always known, but my mother wouldn't listen."

"I didn't know until today." His eyes narrowed. "You're the one who took the stones all those years ago?"

"Yes."

Approval lit his eyes. "A wise thing to do."

"At the time, I thought it was my only choice, the only way to keep them out of his hands, but I know better now."

"What will you do?"

"The stones of Orisis must be destroyed in the Temple of the Ancients. It's the only way. But I have to get the stones, Findris. Rith has three. The Sitheen have the other four. And I've managed to retrieve none of them."

"I may be able to get my hands on Rith's three."

"How?"

A flicker of amusement lit his face. "The power from the three is masking that of the others. He sent all of us to search for them and told us to meet him at midnight. If none have been successful in locating the others, he intends to hand the three over to me so he can get a clear reading on the others." His brows puckered. "The question is, how do we get the others?"

"I'd hoped you might have an answer for that."

He gave her a wry look. "I've had no better luck sensing them than Rith has, and I haven't been hampered by the scent of the three. I don't know where they are."

"I do. At least in general."

His eyes flared. "Where?"

"The Sitheen guard them. But, Findris, I don't want the Sitheen harmed. They were the ones who freed me from the Forest of Nightmares, hoping I would seal the gates again. They seek only to protect themselves."

"Understandable, but misguided, Princess. The gates cannot all be sealed. Did you tell them that?"

"No. I've tried to get them to give me the stones and they've refused. They guard them zealously, waiting for the full moon. Once they realize I won't seal the gates, I'm not sure what they'll do. I don't think they'll harm me, but I'm afraid they'll imprison me as they seek another way."

"Then the only choice is to take the stones by force."

"To kill the Sitheen. I know."

"I'm sorry, Princess. War is never kind and there's far too much at stake to try to protect the fragile lives of a few stubborn humans."

If they failed, millions would suffer and die, including the very ones she sought to spare. She leaned back against the brick wall behind her, closing her eyes against the weight bearing down on her then, taking a deep breath, she opened her eyes and straightened, resigned and determined.

"You're right, of course. All that can matter is stopping Rith."

Pain lanced his foot as Harrison hobbled down the icy, snow-covered sidewalk in the direction he'd seen Ilaria go. Where was she, dammit? Voices carried to him above the sound of traffic, whispered on the frigid wind.

One of them was Ilaria's. He was almost certain.

Pulse pounding in his ears, he followed the snatches of sound through the cold night, along the building to an alcove. Ilaria's voice carried clearly, accompanied by another, deeper one. Harrison pressed back against the brick and listened.

"How are we going to find them?" the male asked.

"The remaining three stones of Orisis are at Bolling Air Force Base." Ilaria's words capsized his heart. "The draggon stone was at Fort McNair, but the Sitheen moved it."

Harrison felt the words like a blade. His mind throbbed with an icy cold that had nothing to do with the weather.

Betrayal.

"I can find it," she continued. "I'm certain of that, now. The Sitheen are guarding the dark stones, waiting for Rith and his guards to show up, hoping to kill them."

His stomach cramped. He felt like he was going to vomit. With a hand vibrating from shock, he dug into his pocket, thick fingers closing around the lighter. Fury lifted its head in his mind and roared.

"They might well succeed, Findris. These humans are very dangerous. To all of us."

She'd played him. Made him think he could trust her. Made him care for her.

He wanted to hurt her, to make her suffer for enchanting him, for lying to him, for making him feel so deeply that he could barely breathe past the pain of her treachery.

"I have a plan. I'll get those stones, Princess."

"We've not much time, Findris."

Pulling the lighter out of his pocket, he stepped forward. As he rounded the corner, two pale faces swiveled toward him—one ivory, one stark white. He barely glanced at the male. All he could see was Ilaria.

Betrayal.

Her mouth formed an *O* as she stared at him. In those eyes he'd once tumbled into, he saw dismay and a soft, aching regret that shot arrows through his heart. Even as it bled, his heart whispered, *You know her. You love her. She isn't evil.*

But his fingers clenched hard around the lighter in his hand. His thumb moved to the wheel and flicked.

Ilaria's gaze dropped to the small flame glowing at his side, her cheeks turning as white as the snow.

"Harrison." She swayed.

Findris grabbed her arm, pushing her behind him in a protective move that drew Harrison's unwanted respect. This one would never turn her over to King Rith.

But Ilaria refused to play the role of damsel in distress. She visibly struggled against her terror to step forward, edging her shoulder past Findris's, as if staking her claim to be the protector instead of the protected.

"Harrison, I'm not your enemy." Her mouth was tight, her breathing labored, as her eyes pleaded with him to understand. "Neither of us is. Listen to me, please?"

He watched the tremors begin to wrack her body and sensed the terror she struggled so hard to control. A terror he was causing. He released the flame and shoved the lighter back in his pocket. The part of him that wanted to hurt her crumbled beneath the misery of her fear. How could he ever hurt her when he couldn't even stand to scare her?

He crossed his stiff arms over his chest, his jaw rigid. "Then talk."

She swallowed. "Like you, I seek to stop Rith. But I can't do it your way." Ilaria lifted her hand helplessly. "I can't seal the gates, Harrison."

The battle in his head fell silent as her words penetrated the aching cold. She wasn't trying to spin some lame story of why she'd had to meet Findris alone. Instead she was flat-out telling him she worked at cross-purposes to him. That she had no intention of removing the Esri from his world. That others would suffer as Stephie had. More deaths, more rapes, forever and ever and ever.

His jaw turned to stone at her free admittance of betrayal. Except…it wasn't really betrayal, he thought bitterly. She'd never promised to seal the gates. She'd never pretended to be anything but Esri. The Sitheen were the ones who'd taken her from the forest, who'd insisted she do what they wanted. All she'd ever promised to do was *whatever I must*. How many times had she said that? How many times had they heard what they wanted to hear? They'd been arrogant fools.

"You *can't* seal the gates, or you *won't?*" Amazingly, his voice sounded almost calm, revealing little of the turmoil inside him.

"Either. Both."

They'd never be free of the Esri again. He'd

never have his life back. All his days would be
spent guarding the gate, hunting the Esri that
made it through.

His head ached, his stomach cramped as anger
flared and burned in his blood.

"Harrison, listen to me. I know this isn't what
you want to hear, but the only way to stop Rith
and any other Callers who come after him is to
destroy the stones of Orisis so they can never be
used against either of our peoples again."

"King Rith already has three of them."

"We may be able to get them back."

"Then you'll steal the others from us."

Her temper flared. "They're not yours! They
were never yours."

"And you'd kill us to do it."

She stared at him, her slender shoulders sag-
ging as if crushed by the weight of his words.
Tears began to glisten in her eyes, tearing a hole
in his heart. "I don't want to hurt anyone, Harrison. Especially not you. But I have to stop Rith
and I need the stones to do it. Over and over I've
demanded and pleaded with the Sitheen to return
the stones to me. But you've refused. We both

know you'll continue to refuse. You'll never give them back to me."

"You could have told me the truth."

"No! I couldn't have. Just this morning you still had me chained. You brought me here to seal the gates and nothing more. But I can't do that. Neither world can survive if they're cut off from one another. One of my ancestors tried to seal the gates once, the *two* gates. The attempt killed her and spawned tempests and storms in both worlds that destroyed vast stretches of land and took untold lives. When it was over, the two gates had become twelve."

He stared at her. What would twelve become? A hundred?

There had to be a way! "Then seal all but one, like you did the last time."

She shook her head. "The draggon stone is, and has always been, the key to unlocking all the gates. Any time it passes through one of the gates, they all open. And the gates can only be sealed from this side. Since I must take the draggon stone into Esria in order to raise the magic to destroy the others, sealing the gates is impossible."

She lifted her hands to dash at the tears beginning to run down her cheeks even as her mouth tightened in anger. "I alone can stop Rith, but the humans won't let me near the stones...*my* stones! Everyone looks after his own needs and we're all going to fail unless we work together. But I'm the only one who sees that!"

Her tears were falling now in a steady stream, but her voice remained strong and passionate. His anger began to dissipate as her words slowly sank in. The gates couldn't be closed. Ever. The only way to stop Rith was by destroying the six green stones.

He met her gaze. Through that cord of connection, he saw that bright light inside her, felt its answering warmth inside himself. And knew she was telling the truth. A truth he didn't want to hear, but the truth all the same.

Hell and damn.

"I'm sorry, Ilaria. We never asked for your opinion, did we? We never wanted it. All we've wanted since the day Baleris arrived was to seal those gates again. To end this invasion once and for all." He pinched the bridge of his nose between his thumb and forefinger, struggling to reorder his tumultuous thoughts. The goal now was…to not seal the gates. Instead, it was to give the stones to Ilaria and help her escape with them. Give them to an Esri…

His teeth ground together. *No*. Not an Esri. Ilaria.

"I believe you, Ilaria," he said quietly, dropping his hand and meeting her vibrant gaze. "I trust you."

She watched him with eyes that glistened with equal parts hope and determination. A warrior injured but not down. Never down.

For the first time, he realized how isolated she'd been. Enemies on all sides. She alone had known what must be done to stop King Rith. But she couldn't do it alone. And she hadn't been able to trust those who could help her.

He saw the aching loneliness in her eyes and felt it in his heart. With a move born of instinct, he opened his arms to her. She hesitated for only a second before walking into them. Her arms slid around his waist as she buried her tear-streaked face against his shoulder.

For one perfect moment, the terrible tension inside him drained away to be replaced by a feeling of utter rightness. Not even the death of his dreams had the crushing effect it should have had. The gates could never be sealed. The humans would never again be safe from the Esri. Then again, if Ilaria succeeded in claiming the throne, the Esri would be ruled by a leader of wisdom and compassion—a queen who might go out of her way to protect the vulnerable and the innocent. The humans.

The tight band around his heart eased just a little. Ilaria would never be entirely lost to him if the gates weren't sealed. He might, possibly, see her again when this battle was won.

If they won.

His stomach clenched. What if he was wrong? What if he'd let his feelings for her blind him to what she really was? What if he helped her take the stones and *he was wrong?*

And what if he refused to trust her and she was right?

As he held her in his arms, feeling her warmth seep into him, he felt his heart ache with the need to open, to embrace her. And maybe listening to his heart was all he could really do.

Ilaria sniffled, shifting her face until the warmth of it was buried against his neck. A second later, she reared back, her face a mask of horror. "You're freezing."

He shrugged stiffly. "I lost a shoe. My foot's a little cold."

She pulled out of his arms, her horrified gaze raking him head to bare toes.

"You're *mortal,* Harrison. You have to get back inside." And in an instant, she took charge, issuing orders, filling his heart with the certain knowledge that she was made to be queen.

"Findris, he needs your boots. Now."

Harrison scowled. "I have one shoe." His expression was mirrored on the Esri male's face, but Ilaria's will was not to be thwarted.

"Now!"

Findris lifted one leg after the other, pulling off the soft unstructured leather boots and tossing them to Harrison.

But Ilaria snatched them out of his hands and knelt at his feet. "Lift your foot, Harrison."

He felt at once ridiculous and unaccountably moved that the true queen of Esria knelt before him to care for his feet. He did as she commanded and lifted his numb, bare foot, reaching for the top of her small head to steady himself. Vaguely, he felt the soft touch of her fingers along his sole as she brushed away the snow, then the firm grip of her hand closing around his cold foot.

She held his foot, not moving.

"What are you doing?" he asked.

"Warming you. Healing you."

And she was, he realized. Beneath her hand, the numbness faded without the usual pinpricks of sensation. Within half a minute, his foot felt normal again, the slide of the leather boot pure comfort against his skin.

She repeated the procedure with his other foot, handing him his shoe, then stood and brushed the snow off her skirt.

"Come." Looking like a fairy princess and acting like a warrior queen, she started back the way they'd come and the two men followed without argument.

Harrison glanced at Findris and the Esri met his gaze, speculation and perhaps a hint of respect in his dark green eyes.

"Thanks for the boots," Harrison said gruffly.

Wry amusement softened the Esri's features. "You're welcome, though it's the princess you have to thank and we both know it."

Harrison glanced at the Esri's feet, so white they seemed to disappear in the snow. "You're loyal to her."

"I am."

"If you're lying, if you turn against her, I'll kill you."

The Esri lifted a single snow-white brow, then gave a nod of acceptance. "That goes both ways, human."

Harrison returned that cool nod. "Agreed."

The Esri studied him. "She has a remarkable ability to see the heart of people, regardless of their race. She cares as much for the humans and the Marceils as she does for her own."

"She's a remarkable woman," Harrison said.

"As beautiful of spirit as she is of face. She always has been. Very different from the queen who gave birth to her."

"I can hear you, you know." Ilaria's softly smiling voice floated back to them on the snowy breeze.

"We're just setting things straight between us," Harrison told her. And while he could be wrong, his instincts told him Findris was a man of morals and honor. All he could do was hope that honor drove him to protect Ilaria and help them defeat Rith.

His gut told him to trust them both. He hoped to hell his gut was right.

Chapter 13

Harrison unlocked the door to Charlie's apartment and stood back as the two pale Esri proceeded him in. Esri. What had his world come to that he, of all people, had to convince the others to trust the Esri?

He shook off the thought as he sat and pulled off Findris's boots, tossing them to the frost-white man. "Thanks again."

Findris nodded.

Harrison grabbed his cell phone, called Charlie, then tucked the phone between his ear and shoulder as he dug a pair of Timberland boots out of Charlie's closet, found thick wool socks, and pulled them on.

"Yo," Charlie said.

"Any sign of Rith?" Harrison asked his brother.

"None. We're taking shifts patrolling so we don't all turn into snow monsters. Where are you?"

"In your apartment. With two Esri."

Silence. "Two?"

"Ilaria and Findris."

Charlie's voice turned to granite. "You need help?""No. Not the kind you mean. But there's been a change of plans." He outlined Ilaria's revelations—the need to destroy the stones of Orisis and the inability to seal the gates for fear of triggering Armageddon in truth. "When I give the word, I want you to meet us at the Dupont Circle fountain with the draggon stone and the other three green stones. It's the only way, Charlie."

His explanation was met with silence.

"You still there, little brother?"

"I'm here and I heard you, I'm just having a hard time deciding whether you've been enchanted, or you're an Esri mimicking my brother's voice."

"I'd answer you with a smart-aleck comment except that I'd be wondering the same thing if I were in your shoes. Ilaria finally confided in me. Up until now, she's been afraid to admit the truth of her mission, that she needs to take the stones back to Esria in order to destroy them."

"Can't say I blame her. Why would we trust any Esri to that extent? Except Kade. Sorry, Kade," Charlie said, his voice away from the phone for a moment. When he returned, his tone was brittle. "You're thinking with your cock, brother, not your brain. Since when do you trust an Esri that much, Harrison?"

Since I fell in love with one.

"I trust her, Charlie. Right or wrong, I trust her."

Silence again. "You've fallen for her." There was disbelief in his words. And wonder. "Head-over-heels fallen. I knew it. I saw it when you were at Fort McNair, when she came into her power. You couldn't take your eyes off one another."

Harrison let out a huff of air. "I'm not denying it."

"Still, how do you know she hasn't done this to you?"

"How do you know Tarrys hasn't woven some spell over you?" Harrison countered.

"Of course Tarrys wove a spell over me, but nothing intentional or malicious. Love's just like that. I think." That stark silence again. "Jesus, Harrison. You're in love with Princess Ilaria."

Harrison's gaze jerked to Ilaria. She had her back to him, watching out the window, but he suspected she heard. She always seemed to hear both sides of his telephone conversations.

"I trust her, Charlie. I believe her only agenda is to stop Rith, and the only way for her to do that is to destroy the green stones, or as many of them as we can get our hands on. Enough to thwart the evil king."

"And what about the other Esri?"

"Findris is the only one loyal to her. He's going to help her."

"Huh."

"Tell Kade what I just told you, Charlie. Ask him what he thinks. Because our only choice is whether or not to trust her. And if we choose wrong, we're in trouble, either way."

Silence. "Hell. Hold on."

He listened as Charlie did as he asked, running everything he'd just said by Kade. Then he waited, his breathing shallow, for Kade's response. If the dark Esri said it was all a lie, he didn't know what he was going to do.

"He's speaking of legends from long past. More than fifteen thousand years."

Kade's voice carried through the phone from a distance. "Storms and quakes like Esria had never seen resulted in the multiplying of the gates. But I'd never heard the reason for it."

"So you think she could be telling the truth, Kade?" Charlie asked.

Kade's response was slow in coming, but his voice was deep and thoughtful when he replied. "Yes. What she says could well be true from the few things I know about those stones. There has never been any darkness in Princess Ilaria, Charlie. If she says this is the only way to stop King Rith, I believe her."

The tension in Harrison's neck eased. He sensed Charlie was back on the phone, but he wasn't talking.

"So?" Harrison prompted.

"It's a hell of a risk," Charlie muttered.

"It's a risk either way. If she's right and we ignore her…"

"We're hosed." He swore under his breath. "Okay, I guess we're trusting the princess. So what's the plan?"

The last of the knots in Harrison's shoulders loosened and fell away. "According to Findris, Rith's having trouble finding the other stones. The power of the three he has is masking the scent of the others. They're due to meet at midnight. If Rith still doesn't have a lock on the others, he's handing over the first three to the head of his guard—Findris—while he searches for the others."

"Which he'll find quickly once they're not masking the scent."

"Correct. But there's something more. Findris is a stone scenter, which means he can draw power from those stones, if nothing close to the power Rith can call. Findris may be able to open the gates without waiting for the full moon."

"Tonight?" Charlie asked.

"No. It's too risky for them to try to go through

the gate here with Rith so close." Harrison's gaze slid over Ilaria's slender back as she continued to stare out the window. Findris sat on one of the chairs, appearing at once comfortable and alert. "Once Findris gets the three stones from King Rith, I want to get him, Ilaria and the seven stones on a plane, out of King Rith's reach. We'll get them to one of the other gates—maybe Stonehenge. Assuming Rith can even follow them, he'll be too late to stop them."

"Not a bad plan, except for one thing. Have you looked at a weather report? This snow is turning into a blizzard. The latest prediction is close to two feet. Everything's grounded for at least the next twenty-four hours."

Harrison groaned. "Then we're going to have to open the gate at Dupont Circle, send Ilaria and Findris through with the stones and then make damn sure King Rith doesn't follow before it closes again."

Thick silence permeated the line. Harrison could almost hear the wheels turning in his brother's head as Charlie digested everything. Finally, Charlie made a sound in his throat, half grunt, half growl. "I'll put things in motion on this end. Call when it's time to roll."

"Thanks, little brother."

"Watch your back, Harrison."

As Harrison hung up, Ilaria turned to face him. "Thank you."

He nodded, feeling the need to take her into his arms. Instead, he turned to Findris. "How much of that did you hear?"

The Esri male frowned. "Enough."

"What's the matter?" Harrison demanded.

Findris's mouth tightened. "I've never held the stones of Orisis before. I've never tried to call their power."

"Rith sent a stone scenter after the stones when Kade arrived a couple of months ago," Harrison told them. "He was able to use them to force open the gates."

"That doesn't mean I can."

"You must, Findris." Ilaria's words were a command.

The Esri's mouth kicked up on one side. "Then I will, Princess." But the worry didn't leave his eyes and wouldn't, Harrison suspected. Not until that gate was open. And Rith wasn't likely to give him much time to do it.

They were going to be in for one hell of a battle. Again.

Findris sketched Ilaria a bow. "I must take my leave. The meeting with Rith takes place soon. I'll contact you as soon as I have the stones."

"You have a cell phone?" Harrison asked. The thought seemed ridiculous, yet with the ability the Esri had of learning all a human knew with a single touch—and procuring whatever they wanted with a bit of enchantment—it made perfect sense that he would.

"I do." Findris looked at Ilaria, some silent question passing between them.

Ilaria met Harrison's gaze. "I acquired some ability to communicate telepathically when I came into my power. It's how I told Findris that I needed to meet with him." She turned back to Findris. "But I'm not sure how far it will work."

Harrison shook his head, feeling a little like he'd fallen through the rabbit hole into Wonderland. Every time he turned around, the ground beneath his feet shifted. It was a good thing he was learning to shift with it.

"Let me give you my cell number," he told the Esri. "Just in case you can't talk to Ilaria…your way."

Harrison rattled off his number. Findris typed it into his phone, then sketched Ilaria another bow and left.

Harrison turned to find Ilaria watching him with eyes deep enough to drown in.

"It'll work," he found himself saying. His arms itched to enfold her again, but things had changed between them. Even if she'd been justified, he knew now that from the moment he met her, she'd been lying to him, plotting against him. Against them all. Planning to steal the stones and run. He understood why she'd done it, but that didn't alter the fact that she hadn't trusted him with the truth—not until he caught her.

That feeling of connection between them had taken a fist-sized hit. Which was probably just as well since she was about to leave.

He took a deep breath and got down to business. "Once you and Findris go through the gate, we'll set up a perimeter to keep King Rith and his gang from following you. You'll be safe from him."

She blinked slowly, a silent repudiation that she'd ever be safe.

The thought of that bastard coming after her later, even if they managed to thwart him tonight, infuriated him.

"We'll catch him, Ilaria. Somehow, we'll stop him. He won't be a threat to you ever again." He was making promises he couldn't possibly know if he'd be able to keep, but dammit, he wanted her safe even if he never saw her again. "Will you try to reclaim your throne?"

Her expression turned pensive. "Yes. I'll try. But Rith won't give it up easily."

Even if the Sitheen managed to capture him, there would be those either loyal to him or too afraid of him to embrace Ilaria as their queen.

"Then we'll kill him."

Her beautiful mouth turned up, but her smile was sad. "I'll miss you, Harrison. What will you do? Build great walls around the gates, I imagine."

"We haven't gotten that far, but yes, I'm sure that's next. Unless you become queen and order your people not to come through them anymore. Is that possible?"

"I'll do what I can. If I get the chance."

The worst of it was, he might never know what had become of her.

He shoved his hands in his pockets to keep from reaching for her. "If you ever need me, Ilaria, come to the D.C. gate, the one in your Banished Lands, and tell whoever's there to call me. I'll try to be there every full moon, but I may not always be."

Her smile turned cocky, rolling his heart in his chest. "The queen of Esria can handle things on her own, human."

He returned her smile. "No offense intended, Your Highness."

"None taken."

Their gazes locked, that familiar warmth moving through him. "I hate that I won't know where you are. Or if you're okay."

"I'll be fine." But worry clouded her eyes and he knew she was as worried about her chances of success as he was. The regal persona dropped away. "We have so little time left, Harrison." Her voice lowered to a whisper. "I'm going to miss you."

Both her stance and expression told him she wanted to close the distance between them, but feared he wouldn't welcome her if she did.

Part of him, the part that hadn't forgiven her for lying to him, didn't want to. But his arms ached to hold her one last time. His heartbeat deepened with a need beyond the flesh. Damn his pride.

He opened his arms to her and she came to him without hesitation. She melted against him, wrapping her arms around his neck as their mouths came together in a kiss that was at once tender and desperate. Her scent wove a spell over his senses as he cupped her head, her silken hair caressing his palm. With his other arm, he pulled her tight, pressing her close against his heart.

If only he could keep her here, just like this. If only he didn't have to let her go.

Her mouth opened beneath his and his tongue mated with hers, tasting, devouring. She was sweetness and light. Strength and passion. She'd whisked into his life like a warm, clean wind, clearing out the staleness and anger, and thawing the frost that had clung to his heart.

Their clothes came off in a flurry of desperate hands and lush kisses, and he swept her into his arms and onto the sofa. As he followed her down, she watched him, her mouth tipped up in that impish smile that promised him his every desire. She reached for him, opening her arms and thighs, and he sank into the cradle of her lithe body.

With a long, slow thrust, he entered her, her inner muscles clutching him in a velvet glove, welcoming him home.

Home. One last time.

Never had he known such a clash of grief and joy. The knowledge that this was their last time lent a tender, desperate edge as desire turned into a storm of need and wanting.

They rode the passion, joining and melding, every thrust driving him deeper into her body, driving her deeper into his heart. Once again, he felt himself falling through that door into her soul, tumbling into a place of brightness and warmth. And love.

As the storm broke over them simultaneously, Harrison felt as if he'd been flung to the stars and back, a rush of such intense feeling, of such pleasure and beauty, he could barely credit the perfection of it.

All the while, he held her gaze, and she his. His gaze. His heart.

Finally, on a sated, shuddering sigh, he rolled onto his back, cradling her against his chest. As he stroked her precious head he wondered, for the hundredth time, how he was going to let her go.

Yet he had no choice. She couldn't stay here. Not unless they failed to stop King Rith. Then maybe, if she had nowhere else to hide…

He couldn't think that way. He couldn't wish for them to fail, not even a little bit. His mind and heart had to be totally in the game. More than anything, he wanted what was best for Ilaria. And what was best for her was to be queen.

Even if it meant she'd be lost to him forever.

With a start, he remembered… *Stephie*.

"What's the matter?" she asked softly.

"My daughter. I wanted you to try to heal her."

Ilaria started to rise. "How quickly can she get here?"

He pulled her back down. "Not fast enough. She's in Pennsylvania somewhere. Hours away. Besides, I'd never bring her here, not with King Rith on the loose. She's Sitheen. One of them might sense her. Target her."

Ilaria curled against him, her lips brushing his shoulder. "I'll come back, Harrison. When this is over, I'll come back with the draggon stone and heal her." She lifted her head, meeting his gaze. "I will do everything in my power to return to heal her. I vow it."

He cupped her face in his hands, feeling the force of her will, of her emotions, and felt his heart ease. And swell. God help him, his life was going to be empty when she was gone.

As if reading his mind, or sharing his thoughts, Ilaria kissed his shoulder again, then slid her hand down to stroke him hard once more.

"Join with me again," she said softly. "I don't ever want to forget."

An hour later, as they lay together, sweaty and sated, Harrison's cell phone rang. He grabbed it.

"I have the stones," Findris said. "King Rith is now following the scent of the others. We've not much time."

"How far are you from the gate?"

"A couple of blocks."

"Good. Stay there until I call you. We'll pick you up." He didn't want the others thinking Findris was one of the bad guys. He hung up and speed-dialed Charlie. As he waited for his brother to pick up, his gaze caressed the beautiful woman now lying on the bed beside him, her skin glowing in the moonlight like marble, a shadow of a smile curving her full mouth.

"Yo."

"Findris has the three stones King Rith stole. Get the other four and meet us in Dupont Circle. ASAP."

"Roger that. We'll meet you in twenty. Oh, and Harrison, grab the two Hokie ball caps out of my closet and give them to Ilaria and her friend to wear. I've issued orders that Esri wearing Virginia Tech hats are allies, not enemies."

Harrison snorted. "Good thinking, little bro. Bizarre. But good."

Charlie echoed the snort. "What about this situation *isn't* bizarre?"

"Good point. VT hats it is."

Twenty minutes later, Ilaria stepped out of the warm taxi and into the cold wind, Harrison's hand tight around hers. Findris climbed out behind her wearing the maroon ball cap with the orange VT.

Snow whipped and swirled about her like a white cloak, stinging her cheeks and tangling in her eyelashes. Ahead, in what appeared to be a small grassy park rimmed by a road, chaos reigned. No, not chaos, but a frantic frenzy of effort by dozens of humans. Some set up spotlights, others directed and drove a line of large trucks, parking them end to end in a perfect circle around the huge marble chalice rising from the center of the park.

Tension twisted into a hard coil beneath her sternum, dragonflies darting about inside her stomach. But it was the sight of the humans in police uniforms, humans holding flamethrowers, that sent a stark chill through her.

Harrison's hand squeezed hers. "The cops will guard the perimeter outside the wall of trucks and try to keep the Esri from coming through."

"They wear holly?" If not they would be all too easily enchanted.

"Absolutely. It's always a risk letting the Esri near enchantable humans, but we need the manpower and there aren't enough of us who can't be enchanted. The Sitheen and Kade will be inside the wall of trucks, protecting you two."

The wind flipped up Findris's ball cap and he slammed it back down on his head before it flew off. Her own hat—the same dark red with the word *HOKIES* across the front—was protected by the hood of the poncho Harrison had convinced her to don again. Beside her, Harrison wore gloves and a parka he'd found in one of Charlie's closets, the fur-trimmed hood nearly obscuring his face. He slid his arm around her shoulders, holding her close as he steered her toward the thick gathering of humans.

Rith would come. Too soon, he'd come. And

she felt that threat like ghostly fingers playing along her spine, lifting the hair at the nape of her neck.

"Where's the gate?" Ilaria asked.

"I'll show you." Harrison led them through a narrow gap between two trucks and into the open area at the center of the park—a wide cement circle rimmed by a low ring of hedges and wooden park benches from the center of which rose the magnificent marble fountain. Hastily erected spotlights lit the area as bright as day, illuminating the life-size statues carved into the pedestal.

Harrison pointed to the marble chalice. "The gate lies there—smack-dab in the middle of the Dupont Circle fountain."

A gate that she'd likely soon be going through, leaving Harrison behind to fight her enemies. And all too probably to die. The thought tore a hole in her heart and she pushed it aside. Now wasn't the time to dwell on such things. Taking a shaky breath, she fought back the emotions that threatened to derail her. There would be time later, an eternity, to think about him. To miss him. To mourn him. Right now, she had to concentrate on her mission or all their lives were forfeit.

Her muscles quivered with the need to move, to run. To fly through the gate, stones in hand, before Rith caught her. Before all was lost.

Harrison's phone rang. "We're just driving up," Charlie said through the receiver. "We have the four."

"Then we're good to go," Harrison replied. He disconnected the call, doubt shadowing his face.

Ilaria knew he wondered if he did the right thing handing the seven stones over to an Esri he barely knew. His gaze swung to her, his eyes confirming what she already knew. He did it for her. He'd laid his trust firmly in her hands and she would do everything in her power to ensure that trust wasn't misplaced.

But so many things could go wrong.

Findris turned to her. "King Rith and most of his guards rode to the Banished Lands, Princess. Two slaves were left behind to care for the horses. Fifteen of them. We mustn't leave any of the steeds behind or they'll catch us too quickly."

"That's good." Excellent, in fact. She'd been desperately worried about outrunning her pursuers if the Sitheen failed to keep them from coming through the gate, but it wouldn't be a problem as long as they escaped with the horses in time.

A rush of power tripped over her skin, the draggon stone calling to her. A moment later, Charlie appeared in the gap between the trucks, followed closely by the other Sitheen. All were dressed in armor…riot gear they called it…and Charlie was carrying an extra set. He tossed it to Harrison, eyeing Findris with wariness.

But Kaderil, who accompanied Charlie, greeted Findris with unexpected warmth. "I've always believed you to be a man of courage and honor, Findris. I'm glad to see I wasn't wrong."

Findris dipped his head in thanks. "I long ago positioned myself to be of the utmost help to Princess Ilaria when the time came." His gaze skimmed the others. "My undying gratitude to you for freeing her when we couldn't find a way to reach her ourselves."

Jack glanced at Kaderil then back at her. Tension lined his face as he slowly handed Findris a small bag. "Here are the rest of the stones. I think you'd better get started."

Findris opened the pouch and poured the contents into his hand—the remaining three green stones of Orisis and the blue teardrop-shaped draggon stone on the silver chain.

The latter called to her. It was all she could do not to snatch it from Findris's hand and place it around her neck. But he was the one who needed it now to open the gate.

Harrison, now dressed as the others, put his arm around her and squeezed her shoulder as if he sensed the battle raging inside her. And maybe he did.

Findris lifted the draggon stone over his head, then moved away, laying the six pale green stones of Orisis on the cement, equally spaced around the base of the fountain. As he placed the last of the stones, Findris began to chant. In moments, if this worked, the gate would open. She'd be leaving. If things went poorly, she might never return.

She turned to Harrison at the same moment

he turned to her. His hands caressed her shoulders, his eyes filling with the grief that tore at her heart.

"I'm going to miss you." His words low and husky, he bent toward her even as she lifted her face for his kiss, hungry to taste him one last time. In the blowing snow he gave her a kiss of such tenderness, such sweetness, that she felt tears burn behind her eyes and it was all she could do to hold them back.

"Be careful, Harrison." *I love you.* The words sang only in her head for they served no purpose but to strengthen a bond that should never have been created in the first place. Her heart might recognize him as her mate, but they were from two worlds, two different races. One immortal, one all too mortal. They'd never had a future and they both knew it.

Findris's chanting carried low and steady over the odd stillness of the inner park. The promise of magic fluttered over her skin. Harrison pulled her into his arms and she clung to him, feeling his warmth wrap around her.

A minute passed, then another as she waited

for the blast of power that told her the gates had opened.

Another minute passed.

Ilaria straightened, pulling out of Harrison's embrace to turn to Findris. Her old friend looked up at her, his mouth a thin line, misery in his eyes.

"It's not working. I don't have the power."

Ilaria started toward him. "Perhaps if I—"

"Esri!" The shout sounded from outside the ring of trucks.

Her heart leaped into her throat, her pulse pounding. *Not yet, not yet, not yet.* She grabbed her skirts and ran toward Findris.

A crack of thunder exploded, the ground shaking violently beneath her as power rushed over her flesh, a foul energy that stung and stank of dark decay.

On the ground, lights began to glow like tiny suns. No, not lights…*the stones of Orisis.* As one, they shot into the air and began to chase one another in a circle high above the fountain. Faster and faster they flew until they appeared to be little more than a single ring of light.

The grim look on Findris's face told her this wasn't his doing. "King Rith has commandeered the power."

Maybe not all of it. Her hand shot out as she reached him. "Give me the draggon stone."

Findris yanked the stone from around his neck and placed it over hers. The moment the weight of the stone settled against her chest, the royal energy rushed through her, sinking deep into her blood. Then just as suddenly, the power turned on her, seizing her mind in a painful grip.

A grip she knew to be Rith's.

"Ilaria!" Harrison's voice came at her from an unnatural distance.

A roaring filled her ears, then rushed away, sweeping her feet out from under her and pulling her into its dangerous current. She struggled to hold on, to fight the pull, but the power aligned against her was too strong. Rith's power. In a blazing rush of pain, she tumbled into darkness.

Chapter 14

Harrison fell to his knees in the snow beside Ilaria. Frantically, he searched for her pulse and found it strong and steady. His own heart started to beat again.

"Ilaria?" He patted her face, looking up at Findris. "What happened?"

The Esri looked as confused as Harrison felt. "I don't know. The draggon stone should never turn against its queen. This has to be Rith's doing."

The hair on Harrison's nape rose, the taste in his mouth turning odd. "What...?"

An invisible hand lifted him off his feet and flung him backward to crash onto the hard, snowy ground. The wind slammed out of his lungs on a whoosh and for a startled moment he couldn't breathe. When he could, he pushed to his feet to find the others rising as well, even Findris, as if they'd all been thrown, tossed in different directions. No, in the same direction—away from the fountain.

All but Ilaria, who remained exactly as he'd left her, prone and unconscious.

Startled gasps and groans sounded across the park.

"What the hell was that?" Charlie demanded.

Harrison pushed to his feet and lunged toward Ilaria, crashing, suddenly and painfully, into nothing. A wall. A solid, invisible wall. His eyes stung as if his nose were broken. Hell, maybe it was.

He had to reach her!

Like a blind man feeling his way, he palmed the invisible surface, seeking a hole or a door or an end. He had to get through.

"Ilaria!" She didn't stir.

Charlie joined him, reaching out a hand, slamming against the same barrier. "What is this thing? It's like a force field."

Around them, the others tried to find a way

through, reaching high and low, circling the fountain.

Harrison turned to Findris. "How is Rith doing this?"

"I don't know. I've never seen anything quite like it." His gaze flicked behind Harrison and he went stock-still, his face paling, if a man with skin as white as snow could turn pale. *"King Rith."*

"Hell," Jack muttered.

Harrison whirled, his stomach sinking, hatred choking him as he looked upon the evil king for the first time, watching as Rith stepped between two of the trucks, leading a small procession of armed Esri guards.

Oddly, Rith's appearance was the least impressive of the lot. Like most Esri, he stood close to six feet tall, his skin the pasty white of toothpaste, his face ethereal, almost effeminate, framed by long, straw-blond curls dotted with emerald beads. Around his slender shoulders, he wore a cloak of gold.

Five guards in silver tunics marched behind him in perfect formation, their eyes trained straight ahead. As if they had nothing to fear from the lowly humans watching their betters pass.

Harrison lifted his flamethrower and fired. A few yards away, Charlie did the same. But instead of flying forward, attacking the enemy, the fire spread as if hitting a wall. Two walls—one on Harrison's side, one on Charlie's, forming an impenetrable path down the center. A path straight to the fountain.

And Ilaria.

Raw panic had him clawing at the barrier as he fought to protect the woman he loved. Would King Rith harm her? Or would he simply take her with him and deposit her back into that forest, where she'd never be free again? His teeth ground together as he beat at the wall, his heart nearly stopping altogether as Rith reached her.

But the Esri king barely gave her a passing glance.

All around him, Sitheen fought to break through that barrier, to reach Rith and his army. As one, Charlie and Jack ran to break through from behind, but the barrier enclosed the army on all sides, moving as they marched.

"There's no way in!" Jack shouted, confirming all of their fears.

"The draggon stone?" Luciar, marching behind his king, queried.

"Is precisely where I want it," the king replied, confirming that whatever he'd done to Ilaria, he'd done through the draggon stone. His voice dripped with ice, sending a chill down Harrison's spine. He'd faced Esri evil before—Baleris, those who'd raped the young women, those who'd murdered humans by the dozens. But all that paled in comparison to the darkness crawling over his skin, now.

At the base of the fountain, Rith stopped, his guards fanning out behind him as he lifted his hands into the air and began to chant.

Another burst of energy skated over Harrison's skin, this one without the physical force of the last.

As Rith's chant ended, the stones flew into his waiting palms.

"He's opened the gate." Findris's words rang like a death knell.

All was silent as those who would stop him were forced to watch King Rith step into the fountain and disappear. One by one, his guards followed until all were gone.

"Dammit!" Charlie's shout echoed over the park, shattering the sudden silence.

As one, Harrison and Findris called to the princess.

"Ilaria!"

"Princess, we have to go after them. We have to stop King Rith. Princess, wake up!"

Harrison took a running start and slammed against the wall, shoulder-first. Pain speared through his arm, neck and back. "There has to be a way to break through this thing."

Findris stepped beside him, pressing his hand against what appeared to be nothing. "The energy is tied to the draggon stone. And to the princess. If we can separate the two, if Ilaria takes off the necklace, I think she'll break the connection. The wall will come down."

"Which is why he knocked her out and raised

the wall between us. By the time she comes to on her own—*if* she comes to—the gate will have closed and he'll be long gone. She won't be able to stop him." Harrison slammed his fists against the wall. "Ilaria!"

Findris turned to him. "You must reach her another way. You're connected to her."

"What do you mean?"

"I think you love her."

Harrison scowled. "That's none of your damn business."

"Call to her, human. Not with your voice, but with your mind."

"I'm mortal, *Esri*. No telepathic abilities, remember?"

Findris's expression hardened. "Do it anyway. If she's not too deep, she'll hear you."

Do it anyway. "Right." Hell. He didn't have anything to lose by trying. *Ilaria?* He spoke her name in his head. *Ilaria!* "It's not working."

"You give up too easily. Keep trying!"

Harrison glared at the man, but did as he commanded. *Ilaria! Ilaria, wake up. Rith has the six stones of Orisis. You must wake up!*

Harrison?

His heart nearly stopped beating, then resumed at twice its previous pace. *Ilaria, wake up, angel. Rith has already gone through the gate. You have to stop him.*

But the thought of her going after that bastard with only Findris at her side cut like a blade. With sudden clarity he knew he couldn't let her go without him. *We have to stop him, Ilaria. I'm going with you.*

No. Too dangerous.

Then wake up and stop me, Princess.

"Any luck?" Charlie's voice broke his concentration.

He turned to find the others had joined him. "She's hearing me, she's answered a couple of times, but she's not responding physically." Turning to Findris, he asked, "What do I do?"

"Keep trying." But the Esri's shoulders sagged.

"What?" Harrison demanded.

"Once the king and his guard are mounted, we'll never catch them. Even if she wakes now, we've lost."

Harrison's mind leaped. "What if we take

horses, too?" He looked to Jack. "The D.C. cops have a stable."

Charlie held out his hand. "Whoa, whoa, whoa. What do you mean *we?*"

Harrison's jaw hardened. "If I can get Ilaria conscious before the gate closes, I'm going with them."

His brother stared at him, his eyes narrowing. Harrison knew Charlie was going to tell him he was out of his mind.

"I'm going, too," he said instead.

Tarrys stepped forward. "As am I."

Charlie pulled her against him. "It's too dangerous with you still enslaved."

"With the draggon stone, Ilaria can break her enslavement," Findris told them.

Larsen put her hand on Jack's arm. "We can't all go. If we fail, there's no one to carry on the fight."

Jack covered her hand with his. "Larsen's right. We'll stay here. Kade? You're our prime Sitheen-finder, but if you need to go, I'll understand."

Kade shook his head. "As a true human, Autumn's far too vulnerable. I can't take her with me and I won't leave her behind. I'll fight the war on this side."

"Good." Jack grabbed his cell phone and pressed a couple of buttons. "How many horses do we need?"

"None." Findris shook his head, snowflakes falling from his hair. "The horses will do you no good. They'll never be able to keep up with the creatures that have evolved in our world. The royal herd can travel for days without rest."

On the plane from Iceland Charlie had told him how, long ago, the Esri had stolen horses from the human realm. While humans were never able to reproduce in Esria, the horses had. More or less. But the resulting animals were hairless and fanged, like something out of a horror film. Apparently they were different in more than just looks.

"How about a Range Rover?" Charlie asked. "A buddy of mine who lives less than three blocks from here drives one. If he's home, we can have it in ten minutes."

Harrison thought his brother was joking until

he saw the gleam in Charlie's eyes. "You want to drive an SUV through the gate into Esria?"

"Do you have a better idea?"

Harrison turned to Findris. "What do you think? Would it work?"

Findris's mouth opened, then closed. "I don't know. Ilaria's power is untested, but she might indeed be able to get a vehicle through."

If she woke up in time. *Ilaria!*

Charlie grabbed his phone. "One Range Rover coming up."

Ilaria, I need you. King Rith has the stones, angel. We have to stop him.

She wasn't responding at all.

Ilaria. Harrison stared at her, fighting to reach her again through his mind. Behind him, Jack, Charlie and Findris continued the discussion.

"You'll need a ramp to get over the lip of the fountain," Jack said. "And gas. There won't be gas stations in Esria."

"How many miles are we going to have to travel?" Charlie asked.

"Close to a hundred," Findris said. "Fewer than that to the base of the mountains."

"Good. We should be able to get there on one tank if the terrain isn't too rough. With any luck, we'll catch up with them long before that. But we should take a couple of extra gas cans for the return trip, if nothing else."

Charlie's voice lowered and moved away as he spoke on the phone. Jack began issuing orders to his men to move the trucks and make room for the Range Rover.

Harrison concentrated on reaching Ilaria. Despite the falling snow, he began to sweat. Everything rested on his ability to reach her. Over and over, he called her name and talked to her, telling her what happened, telling her their plans.

Behind him, the trucks moved away. Beside him, a makeshift ramp was quickly assembled, ready to drop into place when the barrier fell. But still, he concentrated on Ilaria. Just Ilaria.

The sound of a vehicle driving up beside him finally broke through his concentration and he turned to find Charlie climbing out of a shiny, black, late model SUV.

"How long has it been?" he asked his brother.

"Thirty-seven minutes."

Hell.

"The gate is still open," Findris said, anticipating his next question. "For the moment."

Charlie tossed extra flamethrowers into the vehicle. "I packed us a couple cases of water bottles and peanut butter crackers. It should be enough to tide us over if we don't have time to ask the land to provide us food."

The situation was growing dire. If the gate closed, it would be weeks before it opened again and by then it would be far, far too late.

Ilaria! Harrison closed his eyes. He had to reach her. Talking wasn't enough. Digging deep down inside himself, he found the emotion he'd contained for so long and forced himself to set it free. The need for her. The love.

Ilaria, I love you, angel. Come back to me. Please? Love welled up inside him, overflowing, reaching out to her.

Harrison?

Thank God. Ilaria, stay with me. If we don't get through that gate quickly, all is lost. Rith will tear down the walls between our worlds. He'll enslave your people.

Can't...wake.

Then I'm going to have to go after him without you.

No.

You must move, Ilaria. Lift your hands and take off the draggon stone. He's using it to bind you. Take it off and you'll be free.

I...can't.

Yes, you can, angel. You have to or I'm going without you.

"That's it, Harrison," Charlie said, his voice laced with carefully controlled excitement. "She's doing it."

Harrison opened his eyes to find Ilaria's hands lifting with painful slowness.

Good girl. Pull it off, angel.

For a dozen heartbeats, her hands lingered on the chain, then slowly she gripped the silver and pulled the stone from around her neck.

The air sighed.

"We're through!" Charlie leaped forward, Harrison following a second later as he ran for Ilaria.

He fell on his knees beside her, helping her as she struggled to sit. "Are you okay?"

Her lashes fluttered up, weighted by snow-flakes. "I think so. I'm...groggy."

"You did it." Harrison stood, sweeping her into his arms. "Grab the draggon stone, Charlie."

His brother picked up the jewel, then made a beeline for the vehicle as a couple of Sitheen dropped the ramp into place against the fountain. Findris and Tarrys were already seated inside the SUV as Harrison lifted Ilaria into the backseat next to Tarrys, then turned to Jack and Larsen, who'd followed them.

He handed Jack his phone. "My ex-wife's number is in there. Gwen's. If I don't return..."

Larsen understood. "We'll watch out for your kids, Harrison."

It was all he could ask for. With a nod, he turned and slid onto the seat beside Ilaria, closing the door behind him.

Charlie started the engine. "Seat belts, boys and girls. I have the feeling we're in for a wild ride. Either that or we're about to smash the Dupont Circle fountain."

Harrison clicked Ilaria's belt, then strapped himself in.

Charlie reached back, the draggon stone in his hand. "Is it safe to give this back to you, Princess?"

Ilaria looked up, her eyes already recovering their sharp brilliance as the magic lost its grip on her. "Yes, it's safe. Rith tapped into the power of the draggon stone to set his trap, but that's all. He can't control me through it again."

Charlie dropped the stone into her palm. "Findris thinks you'll need its full power to get us and the Range Rover through in one piece."

Her mouth lifted, her eyes widening as understanding caught up with her. *"We're driving one of your vehicles through the gate?"*

Charlie glanced at her in the rearview mirror. "If you have a better way to catch Rith and his horses, speak now. Or help us get this thing through."

The disbelief slid from her face, her jaw hardening. "Do it."

Jack rapped at the window, motioning Harrison to roll his down. "The damned voices in my head have a message for you. *The hawk that wishes to reach the sun must first learn to ride the wind.*

Don't ask me what it means because I haven't a clue." He stepped back out of the way and waved them on. "Good luck!"

Larsen waved from behind him.

As Harrison raised his window again, Charlie drove slowly up the makeshift ramp, then gunned it.

Harrison held Ilaria tight against him and braced himself, half certain they were going to crash head-on into the marble fountain.

Instead, they flew into chaos.

Traveling through the gate was like flying through a kaleidoscope, the colors shifting and changing against a field of black. As if from a distance Harrison heard Charlie swear. Then suddenly his vision returned as the Range Rover landed with a hard bounce and a lurch, then came to a dirt-churning stop.

"Everyone okay?" Charlie gave a low whoop. "Hot damn, it worked."

Something hit the vehicle just below Harrison's window, drawing his attention to the two wide-eyed Marceils shooting useless arrows at them.

But his gaze quickly moved beyond and his jaw dropped, goose bumps rising on his skin as he took in his first incredible sight of Esria.

The ground was blue—bright blue—relieved only by the occasional clump of blood-red bushes or scraggly, purple trees. Scattered across the barren landscape lay fist-sized rocks of brilliant colors as if tossed by a playful hand. Above, the rust-colored sky looked low enough to reach out and touch with his hand.

"Amazing…"

Charlie grunted as he hit the accelerator and started across the bright blue ground. "Not quite what we're used to, is it?"

"Is all of Esria like this? So…colorful?"

"Yes." Ilaria twined her fingers with his where his hand rested on her shoulder. "Our land is more colorful than yours, but I've always found the human realm more beautiful, especially in the summer, with splashes of color against the vibrant green and blue."

He brushed his cheek over her hair, pulling her tight against him as something in the sky caught his attention. Craning his neck, he watched the oddest bird he'd ever seen fly over the vehicle. With green and white stripes, black wings and a long, whiplike body, it didn't look like a bird at all. It looked like…

"A winged snake." Ilaria leaned into him, peering out the window beside him. "They're quite common."

The SUV hit a rut and Harrison held on as the vehicle rumbled across the uneven terrain. He was starting to feel a little off. A little nauseous yet…not. Probably just a side effect from the trip through the gate.

He glanced at the rearview mirror, catching Charlie's eye. "Any sign of Rith and his goons?"

"No." Charlie steered around another of the red bushes, his hands tight and sure on the wheel as if he'd traversed ground like this many times. With his special ops background, maybe he had. "No one leaves tracks in this place. The flowers sprout to cushion your footfalls…or tires…then disappear again as soon as you pass."

Harrison's brows drew together. "What do you mean?"

"Look behind us."

He turned, his brows dipping lower as he tried to make sense of the parallel lines of bright pink flowers the exact widths of the tires stretching out behind the car about six yards. A steady six yards even though the vehicle continued to move forward. The flowers were disappearing, just as Charlie said.

Bizarre. "What else did you fail to mention?"

"Too many things to go into now."

Ilaria glanced up at him, a smile playing at her lush mouth. A smile that didn't reach her eyes. "Our world is not like yours."

"I'm beginning to see that."

"I wish I could show you all my world has to offer," she said softly.

"Once we stop King Rith." He leaned in and kissed her gently, but the touch of their lips sent his head and stomach spinning in tandem, and not in a good way. He pulled back quickly.

Ilaria frowned. "Are you all right?"

"Yes. Just a little…motion sick, I guess." But no one else seemed to be and his own weakness annoyed him. He glanced up. "Since we can't follow Rith's trail, I assume we're heading to the Temple of the Ancients?"

Findris turned to glance at him from the front passenger's seat. "Actually, we are following Rith's trail, just not the way you're used to. I can follow the scent of the stones. But, yes, they're leading us straight to the Dark Mountains and the Temple of the Ancients, as you surmised."

"How soon will we catch up with them?"

"Rith's horses are fast. They're traveling at close to the same speed we are and they had a head start. It's going to be close."

Charlie glanced up into the rearview mirror. "You're looking a little green, Harrison. You want to move to the front?"

"No." It didn't feel like motion sickness, now that he thought about it. It felt like…magic. "It's the draggon stone." He wasn't sure how he knew that, but he did. Like a predator attempting to hypnotize its prey, the magic tugged at him, coaxing him to open up and let it in.

"It's calling to you, isn't it?" Ilaria asked. "I can feel it." She took the stone from around her neck and handed it to Findris. Almost at once that stomach-churning craving died down to a manageable twinge.

Charlie frowned. "What do you mean it's calling to him? How's it affecting you, Harrison?"

Hell. He'd never told anyone. He'd been rejecting whatever pull that stone had on him from the beginning, but he couldn't remember why.

"I've always felt something, whenever I touch any of the stones. The green stones repulse me but the draggon stone seduces. Don't ask me what it means."

"Do you know, Princess?"

"I have a theory." Ilaria leaned forward, her arms resting on her knees. A look of distaste crossed her face as her hands brushed the poncho. She glanced at Harrison. "Help me out of this thing, will you? I don't need it any longer." When he'd pulled the poncho over her head and tossed it into the back, she continued. "I've felt a latent power in Harrison from the moment I met him. Then I realized the draggon stone was attracted to him."

Findris made a sound of surprise. "The draggon stone only calls to royal blood."

Harrison frowned.

Ilaria met his gaze, smiling softly. "Exactly. It's said that Orisis, the last king of Esria, once impregnated a human. It was rumored that the blood of Esrian kings once flowed through human veins. I think it still does."

Harrison stared at her. "Orisis died, what… seven thousand years ago? Do you know how little of his blood would flow in any human descendant's veins?"

"Royal blood is strong."

He looked at his brother. "Charlie's blood's the same as mine. Why doesn't he feel the stones?"

"I've never touched the green ones," Charlie said.

Ilaria's hand stroked Harrison's knee. "Only one with royal blood would feel the pull of the draggon stone, but the blood alone isn't enough. The draggon stone chooses the ones it wants."

"What are you trying to say? That it wants to make me king?"

"No. You're still human. And it's already bestowed the power of leadership upon me. But it wants you, all the same."

"In what way?"

Her expression turned thoughtful. "I'm not sure. What happens when you touch it?"

"I feel like someone's literally pulled the rug out from under me, like my head's flipping end over end."

"I think it's trying to share its power with you."

Harrison frowned. In some part of his mind, he knew she was right. Maybe in some way he'd known from the beginning. The stone had told him and he hadn't wanted to listen. He'd hated all things Esri and had wanted nothing to do with them or their stones. But he'd lost that old antagonism somewhere between falling in love with Ilaria and flying through the gate into Esria itself.

"Give me that thing," he said to Findris, holding out his hand. Heaven knew they needed all the advantages they could get. Refusing additional power was nothing short of stubborn foolishness.

But the moment the stone landed in his hand, his equilibrium disappeared, his mind and body flying into a maelstrom of violence and pain. Colors flashed behind eyes without sight. Whistling screams sounded in ears without sound. Blood heating until it boiled in his veins, he tumbled through an endless, deadly nothingness.

"Harrison!"

From a distance, Ilaria's voice melded with Charlie's, sharp bursts of worry and fear.

The spinning stopped abruptly. And then there was nothing.

Chapter 15

"Harrison!" Ilaria grabbed him as he listed forward, pulling his head down on her lap. She wrenched the stone from his hand and threw it into the front of the vehicle, hearing it strike the windshield, the chain clattering to the dashboard. "Harrison!"

"What happened?" Charlie demanded, his voice hard as granite. "Is he okay?"

"I don't know." His heart beat too slowly in his chest, his brow had dampened with sweat. She'd felt his pain, and felt the moment he lost the struggle, falling unconscious. "He's alive. The power leaped at him, but he's mortal. It was too much."

She pressed her palm to his damp forehead,

seeking the source of the damage, lending him her strength.

"Help him, Ilaria."

"I'm trying, Charlie." His heart rate was too slow. Irregular. He couldn't die. Not now. Not like this.

Pressing her other hand to his chest, she concentrated on his heart, on steadying it, strengthening it. But nothing happened. She needed the draggon stone. With its added power she could almost certainly help him, but she feared what would happen if she let the stone near him again. Even if it didn't touch him, if it leaped for him through her, it might kill him.

So she fought for his life through the gift she had, willing him to live.

Finally, *finally,* she felt his heart give a single hard beat, then settle into a steady, strong rhythm once more.

With a shuddering breath, she tipped her head back. "He's going to be all right."

"You're sure?"

She met Charlie's frantic gaze in the rearview mirror. "Yes." Because she wouldn't let him be any other way.

* * *

Slowly Harrison came back to consciousness to the feel of a soft hand stroking the hair back from his forehead, its mate on his cheek.

"Harrison?"

He opened his eyes to find Ilaria's sweet face looking down at him. His body felt bruised and sore, and for a moment he wondered if Charlie had crashed the SUV. But a quick glance showed his brother firmly in the driver's seat. No one seemed injured but him.

The memory of that maelstrom came back to him with a wrench of remembered pain. He pulled away from her tender hands and sat up, his stomach giving a disquieting lurch. "What happened?"

Charlie met his gaze in the rearview mirror, his eyes at once soft with relief and hard with warning. "Stay away from the draggon stone."

"Yeah. Got that." He ran a shaky hand through his hair. All his life, he'd fought for control, disliking anything that even hinted of chaos. Roller coasters, slasher movies…love. He liked his world ordered. And he liked himself in control of it. Dropping into that abyss had been anything but, and he had no desire to try it again.

He eyed the sight outside the windows with confusion. Gone was the endless stretch of barren blue to be replaced by a forest of the biggest trees he'd ever seen, a place that reminded him of pictures of the giant redwoods in California, except that these trees had trunks of aqua and leaves of pink. There was little underbrush and the trees were well-spaced, giving the SUV plenty of room to maneuver around the giants along a ground of deep golden yellow.

"How long was I out?"

"Nearly two hours," Charlie told him. "Do you feel any different?"

Beaten. Nauseous. "Should I?"

"I was hoping the draggon stone managed to share a little of its power with you before it knocked you flat. Guess not."

"Any sign of Rith?"

Charlie shook his head.

"We're gaining on them," Findris told him. "My sense of them is strengthening."

Good. But were they doing it fast enough to

make a difference? Maybe they'd catch Rith in time after all.

But half an hour later, they crested a rise and Charlie slammed on the brakes, throwing them against their seat belts. Harrison looked up to find a village directly in their path. And dozens of Esri converging on them, circling the Range Rover.

His heart sank. Had Rith put them up to this, imprisoning them in a living blockade while the bastard got away?

"Drive right over them." Findris's voice was dispassionate.

Charlie threw him a look of disbelief. "Like hell. They're people."

"They're immortal. You can't hurt them. And we don't have time to stop."

Harrison stared out the window at the throng of Esri who were beginning to surround them. An entire village from the looks of it, though this was like no village he'd ever seen. Men in silk pants and tunics of various colors and patterns, women in simple, long gowns of solid oranges, yellows and reds. All appeared to be in their mid-to-late twenties.

"No children," he murmured.

"Children are rare," Ilaria told him. "Immortals have little need to procreate."

Beyond the people, he could see structures of some kind, though again, nothing he was used to. There were no houses, only platforms built off the ground and strewn with colorful cushions.

"What happened to the homes?"

"There's no weather in Esria," Charlie told him. "No rain, no wind, no snow."

"The platforms are a way to protect ourselves from the night predators," Findris added. "They provide the means to raise magical barriers."

Ilaria touched his arm. "Let me out, Harrison."

He stiffened. "They could turn against you." But as he studied those drawing close, he saw only joy and excitement on their faces.

Cries of "Princess Ilaria!" began to float through the closed windows of the vehicle.

"Let me out, Harrison. They won't hurt me. They need to see me. And I them."

Harrison glanced at Findris, a moment of accord between them. The Esri wasn't any happier about letting her out than he was.

But Findris shrugged. "She's their rightful queen."

With a frown, Harrison opened the door and pushed it wide, then swung one leg out of the car and stood on Esrian soil for the first time. The golden ground beneath his foot had a spongy, alien feel to it. The scents of loam and forest reached his nose, along with an odd scent that made him think of metallic roses. Above him, through the treetops, the sky dome had turned a bright orange.

Watching the Esri warily, he stepped aside and held out his hand to Ilaria.

She placed her palm in his and let him help her out, then moved past him with a regal grace that had his heart swelling with pride.

Those in front fell to one knee, those behind joining them until the entire throng knelt in a wavelike show of loyalty and adulation. Every face held a mix of joy and relief. Nearly every eye held a tear or two.

One man standing in front, a man dressed a

little more finely than the others, rose and took Ilaria's hand. "My queen. We have prayed for your return since the day you were stolen from us." Nothing but raw sincerity shone in the man's face.

"I have returned, Gerdin, but I'm not your queen. Not yet."

The man's mouth tightened. "King Rith has no royal blood in his veins. Nothing but greed and cruelty. He and his guards passed through here not half an hour ago."

Ilaria squeezed the man's hand. "Rith is a Caller and has retrieved the stones of Orisis. Even now, he travels to the Temple of the Ancients to free their darkest power."

The man's pale face turned a starker white. "You seek to stop him with this strange magic?" He motioned to the Range Rover.

"We do." She took Harrison's hand with her free one, her flesh warm against his. "But we need your help, Gerdin. We need a clear path and quickly."

Gerdin's eyes flashed and he turned toward the other Esri. "Make way! At once, make way!" He turned back to her. "Everything we have is yours, my queen. Esria shines upon you."

"My thanks, Gerdin." Ilaria turned her gaze to Harrison before ducking back inside the Range Rover.

Harrison slid in behind her and closed the door as Charlie took off, the Esri parting like the sea before them, waving and cheering and crying, "Queen Ilaria! Queen Ilaria!" as they passed.

Harrison glanced at Ilaria beside him and saw the gleam of moisture in her eyes. She'd needed this, the accolades of her people. The confirmation that they believed in her. That they loved her.

He took her hand, twining his fingers with hers, feeling her heart beat against his palm.

Stopping had strengthened her, but it had cost them valuable time.

Two hours later, they reached the Dark Mountains. Ilaria had been here before, but only once, long ago. Unlike most of Esria, color was nearly absent from these rocky, jagged, inhospitable hills. The dirt was blue, as it was in much of Esria, but a blue so dark as to be almost black.

And the stones themselves looked as if they'd come from the human realm, a dark, dull gray. Only the orange sky added color to the dreary landscape.

"How much farther do you think we can drive?" Charlie asked Findris.

"Not far. The paths tend to be narrow and rocky once we rise out of the foothills."

"How close are Rith and the stones?" Harrison asked.

"Close. If I had to guess, I'd say he's—"

"There!" Charlie pointed. "I see them."

Ilaria bent forward to peer out the windshield. Sure enough, the mounted Esri were visible at last, winding through the rocky paths high above them.

"Arrow range, Tarrys?" Charlie asked.

"Not quite. I need to be closer."

"No problem." Charlie stepped on the accelerator and the car bucked forward over the rocky ground.

Harrison tightened his hold on Ilaria's shoulders, keeping her firmly against him so she didn't bounce around as Charlie tried to close the distance between them and their quarry. The vehicle lurched and skidded, moving too fast for the good of the car, she was sure, but there was too much at stake to worry about an inanimate object. One that would not be of use to them much longer.

"What about now?" Charlie asked.

"Yes." Tarrys grabbed her bow and quiver from the back, then turned and lowered the window beside her. She started to rise as if to lean out, but Charlie stopped her.

"Hold on. The path turns up ahead. You'll have a straight shot."

The Marceil sat back, pulled an arrow and cocked her bow, waiting. As Charlie promised, the car turned into a curve, giving Tarrys a clear view of the gray terrain and the Esri dotting it.

"Aim for King Rith. If you slow him, you slow them all."

Tarrys began firing her arrows…one, two, three, four. All met their mark, three burying themselves in Rith's neck, one in his cheek.

"Extraordinary," Ilaria murmured. The arrows

wouldn't hurt him, but they might stop him for a few minutes.

The Marceil glanced at her, a small smile on her mouth, before pulling a fifth arrow. But as she cocked her bow, a loud pop sounded from beneath the SUV. The vehicle lurched sideways, throwing Ilaria against Tarrys even as Harrison crashed against her own shoulder, sandwiching her between them.

"We blew a tire." Charlie slammed his palm against the steering wheel. "I brought a couple of spares but I don't think we have enough open ground left to make changing it worth the time. We're hoofing it, boys and girls!"

Harrison straightened, his concerned gaze shooting from her to Tarrys and back again. "Are you two okay?"

Ilaria flashed him a cheeky grin. "We're immortal."

To her surprise, an answering smile lifted the corners of his mouth, lighting his face like a dozen moons. Her heart squeezed with pleasure even as his smile disappeared as quickly as it came.

As one, the five poured out of the vehicle and began running. On the journey, they'd discussed their plan and decided it amounted to only one thing. Catch Rith. Stop him and they stopped his evil.

Simple.

And oh, so difficult.

Ilaria gazed up the steep, rocky slope at Rith and his guards being carried steadily upward by their mounts while she and her companions followed on foot. They'd never catch him before he reached the Temple of the Ancients. Hopefully, the kind of magic he sought to raise would take time. If not, they really would fail.

Charlie, Tarrys and Findris took off, quickly outdistancing her. She could run well enough, but there was no denying the full skirt of her gown hampered her progress while Tarrys wore human clothing—pants and running shoes.

Harrison held out his hand to her and she took it, feeling him take much of the weight off her feet as he pulled her along beside him. Still, she knew she held him back.

"Harrison, go on with the others. I'll follow as I can."

A moment's indecision flickered in his eyes, then disappeared as if it had never been. "I'm not leaving you unprotected." No resentment colored his words. In his face she saw nothing but loyalty and a fierce tenderness that swelled her heart and lightened her step. "I'm staying with you, Princess."

His promise burrowed deep in her heart, filling her with the vehement wish that he would do just that. Stay with her forever even as she knew such a dream was impossible. He was mortal. And she would likely never be free of Esria. If they beat Rith, she might, possibly, be queen. If they failed, she'd face imprisonment again. Or death, as her mother had.

She turned her mind to the task ahead, watching Tarrys dart over the rocks, and Charlie barrel his way up the hill through sheer brute strength. Findris followed close behind the pair, his lean body made to run. They were slowly closing the distance between them and Rith although the royal horses took the path with ease. Ilaria began to believe they might yet be in time.

The Temple of the Ancients lay just over the next rise.

But no sooner had she begun to think they stood a chance than Rith stopped, turned and raised his hands. The arrows had already fallen from his flesh, leaving no marks visible from this distance.

Below him, Tarrys lifted her bow, cocked an arrow, and shot. The arrow whizzed through the air, straight for him, then stopped abruptly and fell to the ground as if it had hit a wall.

An invisible wall.

"He's erected another damned barrier," Harrison muttered.

Tarrys shot two more arrows, but both crashed and fell at the same spot. Rith turned and led his riders up and over the rise as Charlie and Findris chased after them, Tarrys close behind. As the three neared the spot where the arrows had crashed, the two men slowed, making their way cautiously, hands out in front of them.

To no one's surprise, they hit a wall.

As Ilaria and Harrison caught up to them, Findris and Charlie spread out, trying to find a way past the barrier, but to no avail.

Findris frowned. "He used the draggon stone to hold the last barrier." He lifted the stone that now hung around his neck. "How has he created this one?"

Ilaria joined him, placing her hand against the invisible wall. Beneath her fingertips, energy flowed like a living warmth, an energy she recognized. "He's using the power of the temple. Since the stones of Orisis were created here, they're strongest here."

"Which is why he had to return to the temple to access their deepest power," Tarrys said.

"Yes." Ilaria's stomach clenched. "Already, he's far stronger." Their chances of beating him had sunk to near zero. "We have to find a way through this barrier!"

Harrison's hand clasped her shoulder. "Tell us what to do."

Hopelessness swept over her, bitter and devastating. "I don't know."

"The draggon stone holds the source of your

power, Princess." Findris lifted the necklace from around his head. "You've barely tapped into the strengths it's given you. Perhaps you can find the way with the draggon around your neck."

Harrison pulled back without her having to ask. Findris placed the silver chain over her head and the stone settled against her chest, welcoming her with a rush of warm power.

Closing her eyes, she embraced all that it sought to give her, seeking a gift she might have overlooked, a way through the barrier. Understanding came to her.

"Within this stone lies the essence of those who've come before. The six kings and queens who have ruled Esria from the dawn of time," she murmured.

"Can they speak to you, as Jack's ancestors talk to him?" Harrison asked quietly.

"I don't know. If so, they haven't tried." But she knew what she had to do. The question was…did she possess the strength to do it?

As she stepped forward, her hands raised as she prepared to embrace the wall of energy Rith had erected to keep them out, a sudden gust of warm wind tore at her skirts and hair.

"I thought this place didn't have weather," Harrison said.

"It doesn't." Findris's voice was flat and ominous. "Look."

Ilaria gasped at the sight of the sky. Above them, the bright orange gave way to a jagged mosaic of human and Esri skies, as if the dome had cracked, with great shards of orange falling away to reveal a vast, deep human sky dark with lightning-filled storm clouds.

The winds grew even stronger, beginning to howl.

"It's starting." Charlie's words rang with doom. "He's tearing down the walls between the worlds."

"Get us through the barrier, angel," Harrison urged at her side. "It's all up to you."

She met his fierce gaze, drawing strength from him as he enveloped her in the warmth of his eyes. With a nod, she turned and placed her palms flat against the barrier. Pain scorched her palms, shooting up into her arms, and she jerked her hands back.

"What's the matter?" Harrison asked.

"He doesn't want me doing this." Gritting her teeth, she lifted her hands and pressed them against the barrier again. She couldn't let go this time. Inside, she felt the power swirling, battling the evil energy.

The pain grew, taking root in her bones until just the act of breathing was torture. The energy sensitized her skin, tearing at her scalp, until even the weight of her hair became a torment. But at the place where her palms connected with the wall, she felt the battle rage, the power of the draggon stone fighting that of the stones of Orisis. Her power was a match for the evil, but little more. Eventually, she would win…if she could hold out long enough.

If it wasn't too late.

"It's hurting you." Harrison voice shared her pain.

"The discomfort is short-lived, not permanent. It's going to work, Harrison. It has to work."

Her voice cracked on the last word, tears

beginning to dampen her cheeks as the evil energies clawed at her muscles, raking them with tiny knives until every part of her body felt as if it were bleeding.

She was holding her own against the evil's power, but for how much longer?

Not enough.

Vaguely she became aware of Harrison's hands pressing against the wall beside her, Findris and Tarrys mirroring him on her other side. But none of them had the power needed.

Her muscles began to quiver beneath the assault, her arms growing heavier by the moment. Sweat beaded on her brow as she struggled. Deep inside, she knew she couldn't keep this up long enough to win. Her heart plummeted.

She was going to fail.

Chapter 16

Harrison watched Ilaria helplessly as she fought to break through the barrier separating them from Rith and his evil. Her pale hair clung to tear-streaked cheeks, sweat rolling down her temples as she growled with frustration through gritted teeth. His own muscles bunched and flexed in a driving need to snatch her away, to protect her. To take her place.

Though they all pressed their palms against the invisible wall, only Ilaria felt anything. He was afraid the rest of them were just window dressing.

"We're not helping, are we?"

"No. I'm sorry, but this is my fight alone. The power only flows through me."

"It wants me, too." Harrison stepped back from the invisible wall, his hands dropping to his sides and slowly curling into fists as the tug of energy became a demand beating at his chest and head. "The draggon stone wants me to join you."

"No," she breathed. "It'll kill you."

He lifted his hand to stroke the pale curls back from her damp brow, the pull of the magic leaping at him through that simple contact. "If we fail to stop him, we'll all suffer. You're not fighting this battle alone, angel. I'm not going to let you."

"Harrison, *no*. Please!" Green eyes implored him. "It nearly stopped your heart last time. I thought I'd lost you." Her voice dropped, low and pained. "I can't lose you."

But he'd made up his mind. What use was his life if he couldn't save the ones he loved?

"Shh, it's going to be okay." He hoped to hell he was right.

Moving behind her, he curled one arm around her waist, pulling her tight against him as he reached over her shoulder.

For a single harsh second he hesitated, knowing it could be his last. Then stealing himself for battle, he brushed his cheek against Ilaria's soft hair and took hold of the draggon stone where it hung at her breast.

The blast slammed into him like a bolt of lightning, pure undiluted energy. Like he'd grabbed an electrical wire. He fought to hold on, though inside he felt as if he were shattering, as if the blast were trying to rip him apart from the inside out.

His skin felt as if it were frying, his body turning into an inferno of heat. Steam wavered before his eyes. His body shook, but he held on to that stone, his teeth clenched so tight he doubted he'd ever be able to pry them apart again.

He. Would. Not. Die.

The energy raced through his body, through his veins, attacking him. He fought to hold on, certain that if he let go, he'd fly into a million pieces. Far beyond himself he sensed a warmth, a strength, as if the sun itself were calling him.

From deep in his memory, Jack's voice floated through his mind. *The hawk that wishes to reach the sun must first learn to ride the wind.*

Ride the wind. Jack's words suddenly made sense. He had to give in, to jump off the cliff knowing he might crash into the ground, a broken shell.

Or soar.

To gain the power the stone wanted to give him, he had to quit fighting it. He had to let it in.

For one terrible moment, he didn't think he could do it. How did he give up a control he'd clung to with two steel fists for so many years? How did he let go, knowing he could shatter into a million pieces?

The sweetly exotic scent of gardenias drifted into his nostrils, exploding inside his head, his heart. Ilaria's scent.

For her he could do this. For this woman who'd become the heart beating in his chest, he could—and would—risk anything.

Taking a deep breath, he tried to relax and let the power take him. But nothing happened. He was locked too tightly in the battle. He had to let go. Not literally. Not of the draggon stone, at any rate. He had to let go of his fierce control.

He took another breath, letting it out slowly. Then another. And another. Little by little, he relinquished that iron control that had formed the structure of his life for so long. Little by little, the energy broke through.

Finally, on a hard exhalation, those tight muscles that comprised his will gave way. The energy shot through him like a lightning bolt, spinning him end over end in a terrifying whirl of chaos and pain. The kaleidoscope all over again, only this time he'd become the spinning lights as if he'd been blasted into a million pieces—a million pulsing, radiant pieces.

All at once, his physical senses shut down, taking the pain with them. No longer was he flesh and blood, a living organism. He was light and energy. Wind and nature. Everywhere and nowhere. The universe. And nothing.

Lost.

Gone.

For one grief-filled moment he thought he'd died. He'd failed, leaving Ilaria and Charlie and the others to battle an unwinnable war alone.

Then everything changed. He came back to himself in a rush, his blood fizzing and bubbling, strength pouring through his limbs and body.

His senses returned twice as strong as before. His sense of smell sharper, his hearing keener.

His vision cleared, revealing the barrier like an oil spill, plain as day.

"Harrison?" Ilaria held his face in her hands, her expression a mix of shock and wonder. Tears sprang to her eyes, a smile lifting her glorious mouth.

Love rushed up inside him so strongly he thought it might tear apart his chest. He grabbed her and kissed her, sharing his love, his strength, and drawing both in return. The realization flowed through him, rocking him to his core. Love. She loved him in return.

And when he pulled back and stared into her soft, tender eyes, he knew it was true.

He stroked her cheek with his knuckles, his mouth spreading into a rare smile. "I feel like I swallowed the sun and survived."

Her eyes widened. "More than survived it, I think."

"Jesus, Harrison," Charlie exclaimed. "Your eyes are glowing. And your hair's standing on end. What in the hell just happened?"

Harrison turned to his brother, a smile bursting from him, uncontainable. "I'm not entirely sure. But it's time to find out."

He grabbed Ilaria's hand. "Let's open this thing."

She eyed him with excitement and curiosity. "Someone's told you how?"

"Not in so many words. I just know we have to do it together. Put one hand on the barrier, keep one linked with mine."

The wind whipped at near hurricane force as he stepped up to the barrier. The unknown. But this time he didn't hesitate. The power whispered to him, telling him this was what he'd been born for.

As one, they slammed their palms against the barrier.

"Break it with your mind," he told her. Then turned his own will against the oil slick that separated them from Rith. A creaking groan ripped across the mountain, an inhuman sound like a piece of wood straining against breakage. He pressed his power, pitting his strength indirectly against Rith's, and felt the wall beneath his palm shatter with a horrible screech. Shimmering shards of oil slick flew in every direction, a colorful display he sensed only he could see.

"We're through!" Charlie crowed.

Harrison met Ilaria's triumphant gaze, then as one, they turned and ran. Moments later they crested the rise that overlooked the Temple of the Ancients a hundred yards below.

Like the other structures he'd seen in Esria, this one had no roof and no walls. Carved from blood-red marble, the temple consisted of little more than two rings of intricately carved columns—one set within the other. Between the rings of columns, the marble floor of the temple dipped several feet, creating a wide trough.

At the center of the inner circle rose a cone-shaped tower of stairs rising to a round platform some thirty feet in the air. It was here that Rith stood, his hands in the air, his hair whipping around his head. Above his fingertips, flying in a tight, fast circle were the six stones of Orisis.

Harrison's heightened senses took in the situation in an instant—the five royal guards circling the temple, two of them cocking arrows at the intruders.

"Incoming." He slammed his visor down, hearing the click of Charlie's visor behind him as he tugged Ilaria back, blocking her with his body.

She gave a disgusted huff. "Arrows can't hurt me, Harrison. They can kill you."

He knew she was right and squeezed her hand, then felt his own hand lifted to her lips for a sweet kiss. With a smile, he tugged on her hand and together they raced down the rocky path, arrows whizzing past. One arrow sliced across his upper arm, sending a blazing fire ripping through his flesh. Liquid warmth began to trickle down his arm, but he said nothing. He could still run, still fight. And that's all that mattered.

"Let's get Rith," Charlie said behind him.

"No. He's mine alone."

"Harrison…" Charlie came up beside him. "We're taking him together."

But Harrison shook his head. "The draggon stone chose me for this. I need the rest of you to take on the guards."

The five Esri guards gathered in a line between them and their king, two firing arrows as three pulled swords.

Charlie's mouth compressed, but he hesitated only a moment. "All right, then. Tarrys, can you hit their weapon hands?"

"Of course."

"Do it from back here. Harrison, I'll block for you, then keep them busy."

"Good." Harrison turned to Ilaria. Their gazes slammed into one another's and he felt her love flow through him, filling him with strength and purpose.

"Be careful," he said.

"You, too."

Tarrys's aim was perfect, as always, and she injured the weapon hands of all five Esri so quickly she might as well have shot the arrows at once. As swords and arrows fell harmlessly to the ground, Charlie dive-tackled the closest guard, slamming him into a second and giving Harrison an opening.

Harrison took the opportunity, and leaped onto the outer marble walkway and down into the trough. But as he reached the inner ring of columns, a blast of energy hit him square in the chest, knocking him back with a force that stank of decay. And evil.

The lightning swirling inside him called to him. Acting on pure instinct, Harrison lifted his hand and willed that energy at Rith, then watched with amazement as a fireball flew from his palm. *Holy cow.* The king stumbled back, barely catching himself from falling off the platform.

Violent satisfaction curled Harrison's lips.

At the edges of his mind, he felt the magic call to him again, demanding he open himself once more. This time he did so without hesitation, feeling the souls of the dead kings and queens who resided here urging him on.

He pushed forward, onto the dais, and leaped for the stairs. But even as he felt an inflow of power, Rith hit him with a blast that knocked him into the air, sending him sprawling on the marble behind him. His teeth clattered together, the wind knocked out of him both from the force of the landing and the certain knowledge that Rith's terrible power was growing.

How, he didn't know. Was he, too, gaining strength from the temple, or was he absorbing the energy Harrison threw at him, making it his own?

Harrison forced himself to his feet, his back and tailbone aching. Gathering the forces within him, he attacked his opponent with all he had, hoping it was enough to knock the bastard off that pedestal once and for all.

But Rith didn't even stumble this time. His eyes gleaming with victory, he raised his hand and fired.

The blast picked up Harrison and threw him backward into a column. His head smacked against the marble, his vision narrowed to pinpoints of light as he landed in a boneless heap on the marble slab. He willed himself to rise, to fight back, but the pain was too much. His mortal body wasn't built for a battle between gods. He'd come so close to victory. But for him, this battle was lost.

Ilaria saw Harrison crash against the column and go down. A cry escaped her lips at the sight of him, his body lying at an impossible angle. It was all she could do not to run to him to try to heal him. But the situation demanded otherwise. There was no time. The wall between the worlds hung together by the finest thread. Within moments, even that would be gone and the worlds would collide in a violent explosion of magic and destruction.

Even now, Rith stood high upon his platform, his magic tearing apart the sky. Rain poured down in a stinging torrent, drenching her hair and gown as she made her way around Charlie and Findris, who were battling the Esri guards, and into the temple.

The air stank of sulfur and greed, the screeching of the sky interspersed with violent claps of thunder. She had one chance left to stop this tragedy and seconds before it was too late even as the thought of what she must do had her quaking with terror, her hands as cold as a human's winter.

She must call the fire of creation.

While Harrison had battled, she'd found within herself the knowledge she sought—the words to call that mystic fire—and begun pulling that ancient magic through the draggon stone, through her royal blood. It gathered inside her now, ready to ignite. If she stopped to run to Harrison, she'd have to start all over again.

He'd sacrificed too much for her to fail them now. She had seconds to complete her task, seconds before Rith completed his. But she was terrified to the depths of her soul.

Fire. She must call the fire.

It's up to you, angel. Harrison's voice was a soft caress in her mind. *I've done all I can.*

Hold on for me, Harrison. I'll heal you when this is through if you'll just hold on.

I'll do one better. I'll hold on to you. What strength of mine that remains is yours.

She felt it, the rush of strength and the warmth of his love wrapping around her, battling back her fear. In another part of her mind, she felt the walls between the worlds losing their grip and beginning to crumble.

Clinging to Harrison's presence in her mind, her heart pounding, sweat drenching her back and scalp, she squeezed her eyes closed and murmured the words that resided deep in her royal memory, calling to the power of the temple.

The heat of the mystic flame erupted all around her, flickering bright against her eyelids. Terror rose up, a choking, quaking beast that attacked her body and mind, threatening to shut her down, to ruin any chance she had of winning.

Ilaria! Ilaria, stay with me, angel. It won't hurt you. The fire can't hurt you. It lives for you, to do your will. Harrison's voice held her at the edge of the abyss and she clung to it, to him. *Finish it, Ilaria. He's almost done.*

I have to take the stones, Harrison.

Call them, angel. They belong to the flame. They'll come if you call. A deep, violent rumble tore through the temple, shaking beneath her feet. *Call them, Ilaria! Keep your eyes closed and call the stones of Orisis home.*

She did. Using her own strength combined with Harrison's, she lifted her hands high above her head and locked on those six green evil gems, catching hold of them with her mind. Body trembling, she willed them to her, demanding they heed her call.

That's it, Ilaria! They've stopped spinning. They're falling. Into the flame! Harrison's mental voice rose with triumph even as a terrible, unnatural scream rent the air as if the stones themselves cried out at their destruction.

Ilaria wrenched open her eyes, her heart pounding like a drum in her chest. Fire surrounded her, rising all around. A scream built in her throat.

It can't touch you, Ilaria. Harrison's voice encircled her like warm, loving arms. *You don't feel it, angel, do you? Do you?*

No. Through shuddering breaths, she felt no burning, no pain. Only a gentle heat and the blanketing warmth of Harrison's love.

Look at Rith.

Her gaze flew to the pedestal, to Rith high atop the stairs, and she watched in fascinated horror as his face and body began to disintegrate in jagged chunks, much as the sky had.

"He and the stones had become one." Harrison's voice sounded outside her mind, right behind her, and she tore her gaze from the disturbing sight of Rith's destruction to find Harrison approaching, whole and fine. He slid his arm around her waist and pulled her back against him. She let him, settling her head against his shoulder as her gaze returned to the stairs to witness Rith's final moments. Though her heart pounded, strong arms held her terror of the flames at bay.

"As they disintegrate, so does he," Harrison murmured.

"You've healed."

His cheek brushed her hair. "I thought I was dying. Then the pain slipped away. I don't know what happened, but I'm not complaining."

She'd felt the destruction to his body and had been terrified he wouldn't survive until she could reach him.

In a flash of colored light, Rith was no more.

"Douse the flame, angel."

Ilaria closed her eyes, then with a deep breath, released the magic. She knew, even before she opened her eyes, the fire was gone. A relieved shudder tore through her as her gaze rose to the solid, bright orange sky above.

She whirled in his arms, a grin breaking over her face. "We did it!"

Harrison's smile bloomed more slowly, creasing his face, filling it with wonder and love. "We did.

We make a good team, you and I." That smile dimmed, a shadow obscuring the brilliant gleam in his eyes.

He was leaving to go home. Of course he was. And her duty was here.

Tears sprang to her own eyes. "I love you, Harrison."

His hands lifted to stroke her face. "I love you...Queen Ilaria."

She smiled, her bottom lip beginning to tremble as he dipped his head and kissed her with tender passion. Her arms went around his neck and she clung to him, her heart breaking. If she could, she'd give up the crown to follow him back to the human realm. But there was no one else to lead. And her people needed her.

Tears rolled down her cheeks as she kissed him. Deep within her mind a cheer sounded—the voices of her people raised in joy and thanksgiving. Harrison pulled back, staring at her with a funny look, his eyes unfocused as if he, too, heard them. And suddenly, light erupted all around them. As one they gaped at the sight, their gazes flying around the temple. The Temple of the Ancients had begun to glow a soft, warm red as if the marble had been lit from within.

"What's happening?" A bemused smile creased Harrison's face. "I hear cheering in my head as if we were surrounded by thousands."

As Charlie, Tarrys and Findris joined them, Ilaria looked around. The mountain was empty but for the five of them.

"Rith's guards?" Ilaria asked.

"As soon as you drew the fire of creation, they fled," Findris told her. "I don't think you'll have to worry about them—they were followers, not leaders—but I'll keep an eye on them, nonetheless."

Charlie's hand went to his brother's shoulder, his eyes echoing with remembered grief. "When I saw you go down, I thought it was all over. No way should you have been able to rise from that."

Harrison shrugged, a smile playing at his mouth. "I wasn't as badly injured as I thought I was."

Ilaria took his hand. "Yes, you were."

He cocked his head at her. "What do you mean?""I felt it. Your injuries. Your healing."

But he clearly wasn't convinced. "No one heals that fast."

A smile slowly spread across her face. "No mortal heals that fast."

Harrison blinked, his mouth opening slowly, but no sound came out.

Charlie crowed. "Are you saying he's *immortal?*"

Harrison just stared at her and she began to laugh. She took Harrison's hands in hers and squeezed them. "The stone activated your royal blood. It wanted you, therefore it changed you."

"But...but why?"

Deep in her head she heard the cheering change to chanting. *Queen Ilaria. King Harrison. Queen Ilaria. King Harrison.*

Harrison's face flashed with harsh denial and she knew he heard it, too. "This is ridiculous. I'm not..." His expression turned into a mass of confusion, his hands squeezing hers as if he needed to hold on to something solid. "How do they know my name? How do they know any of this?"

"There are aspects of the Esri mind that are

connected. You're part of that connection, now. The race felt you come into your power. They felt your transformation. Just as all know the names of both the dead and the killer if one of us dies, all know the names of those raised to power, to lead."

Harrison stared at her, clearly stunned.

"What are you talking about?" Charlie demanded.

"Queen Ilaria. King Harrison," Findris said quietly, a smile blooming on his face. "The land has spoken."

"No way," Charlie muttered. Tarrys joined him, already smiling.

Harrison shook his head. "This isn't possible."

"Want me to cut you to see if you heal again?" Charlie's eyes sparkled with mischief even as they glowed with happiness. And pride. "My brother, the freaking immortal King of Esria."

Harrison stared at his brother. "Immortal." He breathed the word, as if hearing it for the first time. Slowly, his gaze swung back to her, a light igniting in his eyes of such sweetness it made her chest ache. "Immortal. Like you."

"Yes."

"Forever. Like you." He lifted his hand, stroking her cheek with his knuckles. "You're mine. Forever, you're mine."

Her chest felt as if it might burst from the wealth of happiness inside. "Yes, if you want me."

His arms slid around her waist, pulling her close as a fierce love lit his face. "I want you. *Forever.*"

She swallowed, joy reducing her to tears as adversity never did. "I've waited for you for such a long time."

Charlie laughed. "My brother, the freakin' computer geek, is *king.*"

His gaze still locked with hers, Harrison slugged Charlie lightly in the arm with a grin.

His eyes gleaming with mirth, Charlie hooked his other arm around Tarrys's shoulders. "And all you wanted, big bro, was for things to get back to normal."

Harrison's grin turned wry. "I'd say you don't always get what you wish for, but I think I just got more than I'd ever dreamed of." His gaze bore into Ilaria's, melding with hers, heart to heart.

"My soul mate, mine for eternity." He lifted his fingers to trace her cheekbone as if enchanted by her.

Never had she felt so treasured. So…loved. Never had she imagined feeling such love in return. But there was still a question unanswered. The land had chosen him. But he'd yet to give his pledge in return.

"Will you stay?" she asked softly.

His brows drew together. "My kids…"

Ilaria squeezed his hand. "You'll visit often. We both will. And I'll find a way to heal whatever Baleris did to Stephie." She turned to Charlie. "If you or those you love get ill, I'll come."

The younger Rand smiled. "Thanks, Princess. Or do I call you Your Majesty or Your Highness, or something, now? Queen Ilaria?"

Ilaria smiled, a bubble of joyous laughter finding its way loose. "Just Ilaria will do."

But her gaze returned to Harrison as she waited for his answer. "Will you stay?"

Pained indecision in his eyes, he turned to Charlie. "I can't live without her. But my kids…"

Charlie clasped his brother's shoulder. "Your

kids have their mother. And, hell, you only saw them every other weekend when things were good. Now you'll be able to spend a month at a time. And I'll keep a close eye on them in between your visits, I promise." His eyes turned serious. "Think about it, Harrison. You and Ilaria will rule the Esri. What better way to not only protect your kids, but our entire world?"

Ilaria felt the tension ease from Harrison's shoulders as the indecision cleared from his face. "You're right. About all of it." He turned back to her, joy sparkling in his eyes. Joy that slid sideways, his brows crinkling again.

Ilaria pressed her palm to his cheek with a smile. "What are you worrying about this time?"

"I just realized I'm not going to grow old."

She laughed. "Is that a problem?"

"No." He began to grin, and grabbed her around the waist, pulling her hips against his as he held her captive in the loving warmth of his eyes. "Even forever won't be long enough to love you." In his face, she saw the truth of his words

Epilogue

Three months later

Harrison looked around him with a wonder that refused to dim. He stood within the Fair Court of Esria, Ilaria at his side. The open hall was filled with Esri in their jeweled gowns and tunics, and humans in their suits and dresses. The hall shimmered like a rainbow of silks and flowers, brimming with music and laughter. And love.

Jack and Larsen were on the dance floor, Kade and Autumn sipping champagne. Charlie and Tarrys had their heads bowed together as they shared private laughter.

His marriage to Ilaria, the love of his now-immortal life, was less than an hour old. His heart threatened to burst with joy.

Stephie's sweet laughter rang through the open air as his kids ran through the throng, already hopelessly spoiled by the Esri to whom children were a rare and precious treat. As she'd promised, at the first full moon after her rise to power, Ilaria had returned with him to the human realm to heal his little daughter, bringing her back, whole and perfect, from wherever it was her mind had retreated. Stephie hadn't remembered Baleris or anything after.

While he and Ilaria were in the United States, meeting with the Sitheen, and reclaiming the captured Esri, Tarrys, who was no longer enslaved thanks to Ilaria and her draggon stone, had led Charlie and Findris safely through the Forest of Nightmares as only a Marceillian priestess could. Ilaria had sent them to free her men. Charlie had worried they might receive the same reception as before—a hail of arrows. But all Esri had known the moment Ilaria and Harrison came into their respective powers. Findris had introduced Charlie as King Harrison's brother and Tarrys as Char-

lie's soon-to-be wife, who'd come to free them
from their captivity at their queen's request. All
had fallen to one knee in gratitude.

Now they were all here—Ilaria's loyal companions of three centuries, his own brother and
kids, his Sitheen friends including Myrtle and
Norm. Even his mother had come, her alcohol-
ism a thing of the past thanks to Ilaria's healing
power. Time would tell if such a thing could truly
be cured with an Esri touch, but he was beginning to think there was nothing Ilaria couldn't do.

He caught sight of a young human couple he
didn't recognize doing an admirable jitterbug
on the dance floor. They looked familiar, yet he
couldn't place them. Had Charlie invited cousins
of theirs and forgotten to mention it? He'd have
to ask his brother before he embarrassed himself
trying to introduce them to Ilaria.

Nothing, but nothing, would mar this perfect
day.

His arm tightened around Ilaria's waist and he
looked at her, the most beautiful woman who ever
lived, even more exquisite in a diaphanous gown
of pale ivory, with emerald and sapphire jewels

braided into her hair. She met his gaze, the jewels no match for the brilliance of her eyes, for in them he saw his heart, his soul. His future.

How strange that he'd fought for normalcy, for a staid, controlled life when what he'd been looking for all along was the solid strength of true love. And he'd found it in the most unlikely of places.

Charlie and Tarrys joined them, Jack and Larsen close behind. "We can't find Myrtle and Norm," Charlie said, worried.

Beside him, Ilaria laughed, a music that never failed to bring a smile to his face and laughter to his heart.

He squeezed her waist. "What's so funny? Where are they?"

Ilaria grinned. "They're here."

The cousins walked up, arms around one another, their faces flushed and wreathed in smiles.

Harrison grimaced inwardly, knowing he should introduce his bride.

Ilaria gave Jack a playful swat to the shoulder. "You of all people should recognize your own aunt."

Jack's brows lowered, his expression one of

utter confusion. He looked around. "What do you...?" His gaze landed on the cousins and he froze. His jaw dropped. "*Aunt Myrtle?*"

The woman, a pretty redhead who appeared to be in her mid-twenties, laughed. "I'm surprised at you, nephew. I'm sure you saw me looking not too much older than this when you were young."

Harrison stared at her, then swung his gaze to the dark-haired young man at her side. "Norm?" The man nodded and Harrison's gaze flew to his wife. "You did this," he breathed, wonder lifting his words.

She gave him an impish grin. "It seems I can heal aging. They're not immortal. They're still vulnerable to accidents and sudden illness, but I've healed the effects of aging."

"Can you do that for me?" Charlie asked. "When the time comes."

Ilaria reached forward, squeezing Charlie's hand. "Of course. None of you, or those you love, will grow old unless you wish to."

Harrison looked at his friends, goose bumps rising on his arms. Charlie exchanged a wondering look with Tarrys, the knowledge that they could potentially stay together for most of Tarrys's long life blazing in his eyes. Jack and Larsen looked stunned.

A grin slowly broke across Larsen's face. "I have to tell Autumn and Kade." She whirled away with an air of bursting excitement.

Harrison turned to Charlie. "Now might be the time to find a less dangerous line of work, little brother."

Charlie grinned, hugging Tarrys tight against him. "I was thinking the same." He glanced at Tarrys. "What about accounting? How do you feel about being married to an accountant?"

Harrison laughed. "Navy-SEAL-turned-immortal-accountant. That's almost as good as computer-geek-turned-king."

Charlie grimaced. "It's a good thing I have all the time in the world to learn accounting. It may take that long." A grin broke over his face as he turned back to Ilaria. "It's your wedding, Princess. We're supposed to be giving you gifts, yet you've just given us the most precious gift of all. Time to live and love to our hearts' content."

Ilaria smiled. "You and Tarrys saved me, Charlie. Without your strength and courage, and that of all the Sitheen, two worlds would have fallen. And I'd never have met the man for whom I've waited for millennia. I owe you more than I can ever repay."

She turned fully in Harrison's arms and the rest of the world ceased to exist. "I love you," she whispered, the tears once more in her eyes.

Harrison brushed the hair back from her beloved face, his once-stiff and rigid heart overflowing with warmth and happiness and rich, glorious love.

"I will love you for all the days of my life, Ilaria. You *are* my life."

"As you are mine."

He bent his head to hers, taking her mouth in a passionate, perfect kiss. Around them cheers rose into the air. Stephie's laughter trilled, infectiously.

Life was perfect.

* * * * *

Discover Pure Reading Pleasure with

Visit the Mills & Boon website for all the latest in romance

 Buy all the latest releases, backlist and eBooks

 Find out more about our authors and their books

 Join our community and chat to authors and other readers

 Free online reads from your favourite authors

 Win with our fantastic online competitions

 Sign up for our free monthly eNewsletter

 Tell us what you think by signing up to our reader panel

 Rate and review books with our star system

www.millsandboon.co.uk

 Follow us at twitter.com/millsandboonuk

 Become a fan at facebook.com/romancehq